THE ROX

This is a lively, irreverent and sometimes
outrageous book about eight young people—
four men and four girls—who decide to live
together in communal 'digs' which they
eccentrically nickname the *kibbutz*.

There are Sue and 'Piggy', who work
together in a boutique; Denise who is a
window-dresser in a big London store; and
Olga who tried to be a ballet-dancer but now
works in a solicitor's office. The four men are
as varied as the girls but they have all one
thing in common—a determination to live
their lives with a freedom unknown to their
parents.

It is a story of the permissive society and
mirrors a facet of contemporary living. At
times it is hilariously funny, but it also sheds
new light on some of the problems that face
today's younger generation.

By the same author

Novels

The Lantern Men
The Young Kings
Some Must Die
No More to the Woods
Comet in a Red Sky
The Ruthless Ones
Conquistador
The Small War

Short Stories

The Marble Medici
The Healing Touch

Radio Plays

The Candlestick
More Things in Heaven
The Last Ditch
Montezuma's Heart
All the Trumpets
The Maze
David

LAURENCE MOODY

THE ROXTON KIBBUTZ

ROBERT HALE & COMPANY
63 Old Brompton Road, London, S.W.7.

© *Laurence Moody 1971*
First published in Great Britain 1971

ISBN 0 7091 2021 4

022944

PRINTED IN GREAT BRITAIN BY
BRISTOL TYPESETTING CO. LTD.
BARTON MANOR - ST. PHILIPS
BRISTOL

CHAPTER ONE

IT WAS probably the name—Olga Beloff—that made them all assume at that first meeting that she was Russian. Actually she had a dash of Swedish blood in her but no Russian.

She shared rooms under a sort of co-operative arrangement with seven other young people. They had been exchanging names and when Olga had given hers, Tubby had exclaimed, "That sounds Russian." Olga had laughed and said, "If it is, it must be far back, then." But she saw the idea amused them and for that reason she never flatly denied it. Also, the idea of a Russian girl in the *kibbutz* helped to build up the sophisticated cosmopolitan image they all wanted to live up to.

At first Olga had been taking lessons at a ballet school (which incidentally added a Bolshoi touch to her background). But her toes weren't strong enough to stand up to it, also her money began to run out—though she didn't tell her parents this—so now she was typist-secretary to one of the partners in a firm of solicitors in Moorgate. All eight of them at 32 Roxton Gate rubbed along very well together. There was never any jealousy about who had got whom; it all evened out in the end.

They were a respectable lot, drank only moderately and didn't use pot or anything like that.

There were four bedrooms in the big terrace house. This was a lucky number. It meant that there was never any overcrowding. In other flats across the square three or four people often had to share one room, which was altogether too much and really in a sort of way un-dignified. The rent of 32 was high but not extortionate.

It looked out on a rather shabby square that had obviously known better days. It didn't take a big stretch of the imagination to visualise carriages and hansom cabs coming out from the mews at the back and waiting in the evenings at No. 32 and the other houses to take the occupants to their boxes in the West End theatres and bring them back again afterwards. There weren't any carriages in the mews nowadays. Just Max's old MG.

The names of the seven other young people—to take the girls first—were Susan Bottome, Peggy (for some uncertain reason always known as Piggy) Farthingale, and Denise Mont. Sue and Piggy worked together in a boutique. Denise was a window-dresser for one of the big Oxford Street stores.

The four boys were Ted Allard, who was a minor technician at the B.B.C.; Willie Torr, who had a small weekly allowance coming in from an uncle and could therefore for a limited period have a shot at becoming an author (Willie sat typing for four or five hours each day and as he was the only one in the house for most of that time, he came in useful for taking phone mes-sages and things like that). The other two were Max Rickaby who was the 'London representative'—really a traveller—for a firm that made stationery and typing

6

goods; and ' Tubby ' Weatherstone. Tubby was the only
one who kept changing his job on principle. At the
moment he was junior personnel officer to a small chain
of milk bars. This, he said, boiled down to keeping in
touch with the agencies to ensure that the supply of
waitresses never ran short.

The four girls took it in turn to make breakfast, each
doing a week's duty. It wasn't an onerous part of the
housekeeping because breakfast never amounted to much.
Fruit juice, cornflakes and coffee—that sort of thing. Or
once in a while cheese on toast instead of the cornflakes.
Willie, being in through the day more than the others,
washed up the breakfast things before he started his
typing. Everyone usually got a lunch snack somewhere
near their work, and those who came back for dinner
(or tea if they fancied that) arranged it beforehand
among themselves.

Each room was looked after as far as possible by its
occupants, and Mrs. Williams came for a few hours five
days a week to do anything that had been missed and
keep the rest of the house clean. That was how it went
on, everybody doing something but nobody doing too
much. So far it had worked out fine. All household ex-
penses including the rent were shared equally. Indi-
vidual idiosyncracies were respected but, although it had
never actually been discussed, it was probably taken for
granted that any member who became unable for any
length of time to pull his or her weight financially or
otherwise would just drift off and not become a burden
on the others.

It was Sue who suggested, half humorously, that they
call it the Roxton *kibbutz*. The term *kibbutz* was of
course wildly inappropriate. Instead of being an agri-

cultural community in Israel, this was a community of young people in Roxton Gate. But Sue had been reading about the real *kibbutz* and what it stood for and the idea caught her fancy. So the name stuck.

The Roxton *kibbutz* had been going for nearly a year now, ever since they had all met at that demo.

This afternoon the partner in the firm of solicitors had gone off to play golf and, Olga's in-tray being empty, had told her to take the afternoon off. So she did a little shopping for herself, then, remembering that Ted Allard had used the last of his brushless shaving cream that morning, she bought a tube of that as well. (Ted was bearded but he put in a lot of razor work on the thing, like a conscientious topiarist).

Then she went back to the *kibbutz*. Willie Torr, his mop of dark hair tousled like a sheepdog's, was sitting over his typewriter in the living-room. His face above the nylon polo-neck had the frustrated, fiercely concentrated look that came when his plots got stuck. His plots always got stuck. He had never finished a book yet but he *could* write (or so everyone believed, Olga most of all) and might even one day end up writing well. In the meantime his uncle's allowance gave him time to find out, which is more than most embryo writers get.

Willie, who had boxed at school, had a slightly bent nose which gave him a tough-handsome look. In reality he was probably the least tough of the four men and was given to worrying about life. Writing books is apt to do that to you anyway.

"Hey, Willie," Olga said, putting the shaving cream on the mantelpiece.

8

" Hey."

" Like a cup of coffee?"

" Yes, please. Back early, aren't you?"

" My boss went off to play golf."

She went through to the kitchen and heated a little milk in a saucepan. As she reached for the instant coffee jar she could hear Willie going on about his plot.

" This bloody woman—I've got her in a mess all right. She's a pop singer, see?—not really big time but making a fair enough go of it. Then there's this Johnny who comes to hear her every night. He's stinking rich and wants her to live with him. But in the background she's got a boy friend she likes better. Only he's a clerk and doesn't earn a quarter of what she's making. Most writers would make her go for the little guy—but oh hell, I don't know. Give me the contemporary woman's angle, Olga— what would she do?"

" I'll think about it while I'm making the coffee," Olga called back to him. Inwardly she thought, Oh lord, another hackneyed one.

She poured the cups and put in the brown sugar, two spoonfuls for Willie and one for herself, and went back to the living-room. She put one cup down beside Willie's typewriter and sat opposite him.

" Well?" Willie said. " What would my bloody woman do? With your Slav blood you're bound to know."

" Depends on the sort of woman she is," Olga said. " If she wants money more than a man, she'll go for the stinking rich one. If she needs her man more than money, she'll take the little guy."

" For Pete's sake I know that. I can work out the alternatives. Lolly or nookie. The point is, which would *this*

A* 9

woman plump for? She's a pop singer, remember—"

"She's a woman first. I can't tell you what sort of woman, Willie. You've made her, you should know."

"Okay, okay," Willie said impatiently. "What would *you* do then? This girl's supposed to be a blonde—like you. Good figure, nice legs, like yours. You'd probably think alike too. So just what would *you* do?"

Olga suddenly felt sorry for Willie (as she did quite often). He was more vulnerable, she felt, than Ted or Max or Tubby. This was almost certainly because he felt less independent than anyone else in the *kibbutz*, the girls included. The allowance from his uncle probably worked two ways, like wings to lift him up but also like a weight tied to his feet to keep him from flying too far on his own. Still—there was no use in pretending. You could pretend about things like having Russian blood in you— that wasn't serious. But Willie's plots, or lack of plots, were very serious indeed.

"Oh come on, girl, what would *you* do?" Willie urged.

"I—I think I'd tear this one up and start again, Willie," Olga said gently. "It's—well, it's not very original, is it?"

Willie stared at her.

"Christ, you're encouraging today and no mistake," he said.

"You asked me what I thought. It's no use pretending—"

"I asked you what you'd do in a given circumstance—"

"And I'm telling you what I'd do in *this* circumstance—"

"I meant the circumstance in my book—"

"I don't believe in the circumstance in your book,"

Olga said quietly. " I'm sorry, Willie, but I don't."

" Oh bugger and blast," Willie snapped crossly. He tore the sheet of paper out of the typewriter, crumpled it up and shot it across the table at Olga. She ducked and it bounced off her fair head. She picked up the ball of paper and tossed it into the wastepaper basket.

They finished their coffee in silence, not really quarrelling but with a slight constraint between them. They had gone as far as disagreement ever went in the Roxton *kibbutz*. They liked each other very much without being in love; indeed, none of the eight could be said at the moment to be really in love with any of the others. In the *kibbutz* falling in love as a preliminary to permanent alliance was not regarded favourably. You got your sex all right but you never became so possessive and *bourgeois* as to fall in love, at any rate not with the intention of marriage.

Presently Olga rose and took the empty cups back to the kitchen to wash them. As she was drying them Willie wandered up behind her. It was a purposeful sort of wander. She knew what he was going to do and suddenly she was glad she'd got the afternoon off. Each of the men had a different way of caressing. Willie put his arms round her now, his hands felt for her breasts and he kissed the back of her neck. Even if you'd been blindfolded you could always have told whose arms were going round you. Willie did it gently, considerately. Willie's words were always rougher than his hands.

" I was cross because you were so bloody right," he said, nuzzling her neck. " I try to put too much in. Hell, I haven't learnt yet that all you have to do is write something people will believe in. It sounds so easy. It

11

doesn't have to be sensational—just believable. But I can't do it—yet."

"You will," Olga said.

His hands were still gently kneading her breasts.

"Can we—can we go upstairs—?"

"You think it's good for plots—?"

"I don't know—it's just good."

She was reaching up to put the cups and saucers back on the shelf. If she had wanted to discourage him she wouldn't have bothered putting them up there until later. She'd just have kept her elbows close against her sides and he'd have understood.

"You're sharing with Piggy," Olga said. "Mightn't she mind—?"

"God no, of course she wouldn't." He sounded incredulous, almost outraged. "We're all free—you know that. It's not a bloody monastery. Or a nunnery. That's the whole idea. Anyway, why Piggy any more than Ted? Don't tell me you're still a stinking *bourgeoise* at heart."

"No. But mother taught me it's ladylike to hang back."

"You *are* still a stinking *bourgeoise*."

From the feel of his lips on her neck she knew he was still gentle Willie Torr—but urgent Willie too, now. Quite different from Ted or Max or Tubby. Love came in such varied wrappings.

She turned and put her arms round his neck and they studied each other's faces for a moment. Then she kissed him quickly on his bent nose.

Fingers touching, they went upstairs.

Denise Mont went through the gate of the house at Strawberry Hill and up the garden path. She was a vivid redhead and was wearing a maxi coat in the particular shade of green that went best with her hair. Below her maxi one could just glimpse her very high heels, which were an exactly matching shade of green. From a distance she looked as very small girls, the younger daughters of the top aristocracy, used to look in Tudor times, but from close up she looked a modern dish, a very tasty modern dish.

Her mother would probably be somewhere at the back so Denise went round, crossing the corner of the lawn that ran down towards the river and leaving little marks in it like a sparrow might make if a sparrow could use a pogo-stick. Then she went through the french window, which was lying open that sunny afternoon, and along the corridor to the big kitchen beyond.

Her mother was there all right, chopping vegetables for that evening's dinner and looking more than ever like a younger edition of Dame Edith Evans.

" Hi, Mum," Denise said and pecked her on the cheek.

" Oh it's you, dear," Mrs. Mont said. " I felt sure it was the woman—she hasn't come, you know. If she'd even send word. You'd think they'd pick up a phone. They're really *most* unreliable these days. It must be this Government. Let me look at you."

She held Denise at arms' length and studied her.

" Hm. I must say you look well, dear, and—sort of satisfied. I hope you're not sleeping with a young man or anything like that. You weren't brought up that way."

Denise burst into a peal of laughter. She was thinking with genuine amusement, what do they think sex is for? Like a piece of jewellery you lock away in your

13

bank because it's too good to use? Don't they realise things deteriorate from neglect? Even a car's no good till it's run in.

"What a scream you are, Mummy," she said. She took off her maxi and threw it over a chair. Below the maxi was a mini and below the mini a pair of legs shapelier than any Chippendale ever created. "Where's Daddy?"

"At the office, dear—where else would he be? We didn't expect you again so soon. It's usually a fortnight between your flying visits, isn't it? How did you manage to get away at this time of day?"

"Oh, I'd just finished two big windows on my own —the middle ones in Oxford Street. When you've done twelve hours or so crawling about on your knees they let you off for half a day to recover. You must have a look at them next time you're up in town, Mummy— the windows, I mean, not my knees. I'll bet there's nothing like them anywhere else in London and they won't want them changed for three weeks at least—the windows, I mean."

"I'll try to get up sometime, dear," Mrs. Mont promised. "It does seem rather an odd job though—dressing windows. But if it's what you like—"

"Oh I love it, Mummy," Denise said. Her green eyes danced at a memory. "You get a giggle, too. When I'm crawling about in slacks on my hands and knees I turn my back on the window. Quite often a row of boys line up at the window to admire my bum. It gives you a lift."

"Really, dear—what dreadful, dreadful expressions you use. I suppose your slacks are too tight." Mrs. Mont went off at a tangent as she was apt to do. "Look dear

—I made some meringues yesterday. Put up two deck-chairs on the lawn and we'll have a cup of tea out there —in the sheltered bit under the parasol. You won't need your coat, it's warm for April. I'll call you when I need help with the trolley."

Ten minutes later they were seated together under the big coloured parasol, munching meringues and watching the swans on the river. Mrs. Mont was thinking how pretty her daughter looked—rather like the Myrna Loy of her own youth. (Though was *she* a redhead? In those days there had only been black and white and Mrs. Mont couldn't recall having seen Miss Loy since colour came in.) Only she felt sure Myrna would never have displayed as much leg as Denise was showing at this moment. Thank God they wore tights nowadays—that made it safer. It used to be only ballet-dancers and principal boys who wore tights. Anyway, there was nothing you could do about it. Young people had branched off on a different road from their elders. Just where it would lead them to remained to be seen. You couldn't be absolutely sure about anything, but there was one thing to be thankful for—she felt Denise had too much sense ever to kill herself with these drugs.

Denise started on her third meringue. She inherited from her mother the blessed gift of being able to have a real go at rich food once in a while without it showing on her figure. Mrs. Mont said chattily, " Now tell me about your boy-friends, dear. Is there anyone special?"

"Not really," Denise said vaguely. She split the meringue in two, examined both halves carefully to see which was the creamier, decided it was the left hand one, then daintily licked the cream off with a pink

tongue. "Yummy. Unless you could call Tubby special.
I seem to see more of him at the moment than I do of
the others. But it might be someone else next week or
the week after."

"Tubby—?"

"Yes—Tubby Weatherstone. I say, Mummy, you're
terrific at making meringues—but of course you know—"

"And what does he do?"

"He's a personnel officer or something—"

"That sounds good, dear," Mrs. Mont murmured.

"I don't honestly think it's as good as it sounds," her
daughter said.

"Oh? Why don't you bring him down sometime?"

"He mightn't come—or perhaps he would if you promised him meringues."

"Then we'll promise him meringues. Tell me more
about him, dear."

"But there's nothing more to tell, Mummy."

Denise's voice had taken on the slight edge that always
came when she didn't want to be questioned further on
a particular topic. It was wonderful how today's young
people could run the shutters up in a twinkling. Mrs.
Mont knew better than to try to force them open. But
sometimes you could peep in at another window. You
never got a complete view of anything, just odd pieces of
a jigsaw.

"This *kibbutz* thing," she said casually. "I suppose
I'm getting stupid but I've never quite got the hang of
it. Would you like to tell me something about how it
started?"

"How it started?—oh there was nothing out of the
ordinary about how it started," Denise said readily
enough. "I'd been on a demo—"

16

" A demo—?" (Mrs. Mont said it exactly as Edith Evans in the part of Lady Bracknell in the film had said, ' A *hand*-bag?'.)

" A demonstration. I don't remember who promoted it—maybe the L.S.E. or someone like that. I'm not even sure now what it was in aid of but I must have thought it was a worthy cause at the time. Anyway, when it was over eight of the marchers including me went to a pub to have a drink together. Talk about soul-mates—we found we'd all exactly the same idea about things—"

" What sort of things, dear?"

" For God's sake, Mummy—just things. Anyway, we hit it off so well we all arranged there and then to move into digs together in a house that one of them happened to know was coming vacant—with a shower in every bedroom, too."

" And were these eight people all of—er—one sex, dear?" Mrs. Mont asked.

" Oh no, four of each. Well, it turned out afterwards that none of us had been really satisfied with the rooms we'd been living in before we met, so our meeting was doubly lucky. That's all there is to it, Mummy." Denise smiled and shrugged disarmingly. " We don't aim to turn the world upside down or start a war or anything like that. Anyone who gets tired of the set-up is free to walk out and look for digs somewhere else."

" It sounds interesting," Mrs. Mont said carefully. " Maybe some day I'll drop in to visit you there."

" Be sure to let me know beforehand if you do, that's all," Denise said. " Half the time there's nobody in. You don't want your journey for nothing."

" One thing more, dear—how many bedrooms?"

" Four. Everyone has to share."

"I hope the girl you're sharing with is congenial," Mrs. Mont said. "It makes such a difference."

"Oh all the girls are congenial," Denise said, poker-faced.

"That's nice. Now—why don't you stay for dinner, dear?" her mother asked. She felt there was never enough time to discuss any subject from beginning to end.

"Sorry, Mummy, can't—got things to do," Denise said regretfully.

They chatted on for a quarter of an hour longer, Mrs. Mont mostly listening while Denise animatedly described the sort of clothes that were 'in' at the store where she worked. Then it got chilly so they went inside and chatted for another quarter of an hour in the kitchen. Mrs. Mont did most of the chatting now—about neighbours' daughters who were engaged or getting married and about what they should give for wedding presents. While they talked Denise helped her mother chop the rest of the vegetables and trimmed two steaks which she did as deftly and artistically as she dressed her windows in Oxford Street. After that Denise left to return to London.

Before going she kissed her mother and asked her to give her love to her father. Her last words were, "Remember, Mummy—if you're dropping in be sure to let me know beforehand." She said it quite casually but she made sure her mother's attention wasn't straying at that moment.

Denise was very fond of both her parents though she felt she had outgrown living with them. She couldn't remember ever having had a serious disagreement with either of them in all the years they had been together as a family. But really, Mummy's interests were so narrow and old-fashioned you'd think there was no world outside—and her father, probably through listening to her mother, had become every bit as bad. Denise had first begun to notice this when she was about sixteen, which was nearly four years ago now.

That was the trouble—Mum and Dad knew so little about the *real* world.

Max Rickaby and Sue Bottome were having a drink together one evening in the cubicle of a pub near Piccadilly Circus. They very seldom went out together. Just because they shared a bedroom at the *kibbutz* didn't mean they had to live the rest of the time in each other's pocket—that would have been alien to the whole idea of freedom in the *kibbutz*. But Max had heard indirectly that someone was giving a party in a flat in Chelsea and it was easier to slip in if you went with a girl. A man going singly or a mob of fellows arriving together almost automatically got the gatecrasher treatment. Sue being the nearest girl at hand at the moment Max had asked her and she had said with *kibbutz* casualness, " Okay, let's have a shot at it."

As no one ever went to a party before ten at the earliest, they had arranged to fill in the time sitting over a drink at a pub.

Sue was pretty and trim except for being thirty-nine round the bra, which worried her a bit, but everyone said it suited her and that she could carry it, which seemed to her a superfluous thing to say seeing she already *was* carrying it. (She wondered where it came from; her mother was as flat as a board.) Tonight she was wearing mustard-coloured slacks and pullover and her hair was so long and black it looked like a Cleopatra wig, which it wasn't. Sue's temperament was a thing of contrasts. Although she was probably the most devoted *kibbutzer* of the lot, she was usually placid and easy-going and people who didn't know her very well took it for granted she was always like that. But they'd never seen her worked up about something. Sue making love, for instance, was a genuine no-nonsense wholehearted all-action participator.

The four girls agreed among themselves that Max was the best-looking of the four men in the *kibbutz* and that none of the others was less than passable and, any-way, looks weren't all that important in a man. There was a hint of film-star looks about Max, in the Gregory Peck-when-young range. There was also a hint of copper in his hair, which covered his collar but was never allowed to get further down than that. Max had tried growing a beard but oddly enough it had turned out mousey which clashed horribly with the copper, so he had given up the idea. (Ted Allard was the only bearded one and him it really suited, apart from being practically mandatory in his department of the B.B.C. It made him look a little like Fidel Castro, though he kept it tidier than Fidel's, judging from the photographs of the Cuban leader in the papers.)

Now, over their half pints of bitter, Sue asked, "What'll we do if we don't get in?"

"Have the other half pint somewhere and go home to television," Max suggested. "Or is there anything else you have in mind?"

"No, that's okay," Sue said. "There's a bit of sewing and laundering I can be doing."

It had never occurred to Max that such activities went on in the *kibbutz*. He just put things in the basket and took it for granted they all went to the laundry. The men were never about when the girls picked out the small things that the laundry might damage or lose, and did them up themselves in odd moments. It was just one of the things women did in a mixed community without being asked, just as men moved furniture that needed moving or carried heavy buckets or things like that. Both of them did these things automatically without asking themselves, am I doing more than my share?

"How come I never see you at it?" Max asked.

"There are lots of things women have to hide from men. Even wives from their husbands. All through history they've done it—that's why they're so good at it."

"Men hide things from women too—"

"No—they only think they do."

Max turned this over in his mind for a moment or two and the reflection raised others.

"Now we're on the subject," he said, "just what do you four females think of us four men?"

"We weren't really on the subject. Anyway, how do you mean?" Sue giggled. "As performers—?"

"What else?"

"It's against the spirit of the *kibbutz* to criticise other members," Sue said primly.

"It doesn't have to be criticism. It could be a paean of praise."

"You'll be lucky."

"Oh go on—just in a general way."

"No one makes love in a general way. It's very personal."

"Don't be so bloody awkward," Max said amiably.

Sue took another sip of her beer, considering whether or not she was being bloody awkward.

"All right, then," she said, "in a general way. Willie's the gentlest. Tubby does it the way he does everything —you know how he gobbles his food and finishes before anyone else. He's ready to leave the table when the rest of us are just getting to the best bits. You and Ted are good, honest, dependable workmen. Ted's beard tickles —that's a plus or a minus according to taste."

"That leaves me the only one without an idiosyncracy. Unless, of course, I'm the superman."

Sue giggled again.

"No Maxie, I couldn't honestly call you that." Counter-curiosity had been stirred in Sue in spite of herself. "Maybe you'd like to say a word about us girls," she suggested.

Max swirled his beer round in the glass.

"It'd be against the spirit of the *kibbutz*—remember?"

"Oh come off it."

Max grinned.

"Well, I'd probably give you all passes in an exam if I were marking."

"What no honours?"

"It would depend what you were marking for— accuracy, style, brevity, what have you. I'll tell you one thing, Sue—you're the most energetic."

It suddenly occurred to Sue that they didn't usually discuss each others' qualities like this and that it really could be regarded as a sort of disloyalty to the *kibbutz*. She looked at her watch.

"It's nearly ten—hadn't we better get started for this party of yours?"

"It isn't mine, God knows whose it is," Max said.

"Suppose we'd better take a bottle—what do you think?"

"Yes—Spanish type'll do, it mightn't be much of a party." (Sue's work in the boutique gave her a keen sense of values.)

A list of prices was up at the counter. Before he left the cubicle Sue insisted on paying her half. Max went over to the counter and bought the bottle. He came back and said, "Okay, let's go, my little pouter pigeon."

Sue flushed slightly and instinctively her eyes went down to her pullover.

"Don't be rude," she said quietly.

She sounded hurt. Max looked at her quickly and realised she really was offended. He had forgotten for the moment how self-conscious she was on that one point (or, to be precise, two points).

"Look," he told her seriously, "I like pouter pigeons. You know that—I keep on telling you. If I had a pigeon loft, they'd all be pouters."

Sue didn't answer immediately. Max took the bottle from under his car-coat and set it on the table, as if this was something they must get settled before they did anything further. The slightly hurt look left Sue's eyes. They bent towards each other and touched lips. Max tucked the bottle under his coat again and said, "Okay, then, let's go." Sue rose and they left the pub.

They strolled past Billy's Baked Potato and went underground at the Regent Palace corner. There had still been some light left when they went into the pub, now it was dark. They surfaced at Sloane Square and Max looked around, trying to remember where the party was supposed to be. It was now about ten-thirty.

"This way, I think—I hope," he said.

23

They found it after about ten minutes of searching. It was a big, old terrace house, with peeling paint, railings in front and six steps up to the door. Every window was lit up and the noise of two or more record-players came in gusts from different floors. It had the look of a house that had taken drink and was now belching and considering going to the loo.

Max rang the bell. The door was opened by three young men who had their arms about each others' shoulders like front-row forwards about to engage. They stared at Max and Sue glassily. Beyond them was a haze of smoke, a babel of sound, and a hall solid with young people holding glasses. Some seemed to be dancing but they were moving so little you couldn't be sure if they were really dancing or just standing about talking like the others.

" Max and Sue—we're expected," Max announced casually, but the three were still staring glassily. Max took the bottle from under his coat. " This is what Joe said to bring—though I don't fancy Spanish stuff much myself," Max added. " Where can I find Joe—?"

" Gimme," one of the front-row forwards said, his voice slurring. He grabbed uncertainly at the bottle. " Go ahead, Sax and Moo."

" Close the bloody door, can't you?" someone shouted.

As they pushed towards the cloakroom, Sue asked, " Joe who?" All the pegs were full so they dropped their coats on top of a lot of others in a corner. " How the hell should I know?" Max said. " There's always a Joe. See you later. Good hunting. Okay?"

" Okay," Sue told him. " Don't overtire yourself."

It turned out to be just like any other party, neither better nor worse. A person or persons unknown had prepared sausages on sticks and topped buttered water-biscuits with the usual scraps of tomato, cucumber and cheese. Plates of these lay around in odd corners and under furniture and what wasn't eaten eventually reached the carpet and was trodden into it. In a room off the hall there was something resembling a hip-bath on a table, half full of an unrecognisable liquid. Every now and then as another couple arrived one of the front-row forwards would stagger forward and empty the newcomers' bottle into the hip-bath to the accompaniment of ragged cheering.

Sue sampled the contents three or four times and got into conversation first with a queer and then with an earnest Slade School type of girl. The queer seemed to be talking about witchcraft and the girl about abortion so Sue talked about these things too, but she couldn't be sure that either topic was the right one because of the noise.

Then Sue necked with one or two of the men she fancied and who fancied her, but she didn't feel like going upstairs to where the action was so she didn't go. She didn't see much of Max but noticed him once, huddled in a corner with an attractive black girl. She was beginning to yawn a little and the crowd had thinned out appreciably, the leavers perhaps going on to other parties. But she thought Max was probably enjoying himself and didn't want to hurry him.

The music was still blaring away so that any sort of sustained conversation was still a matter of lip-reading. But there was room to dance a little now and presently Sue found herself facing one of the front-row forwards. He was snapping his fingers and jerking his pelvis in great style. So Sue, partly to keep him company but more because of the effects of the hip-bath beverage, began also to shake everything somewhat more uninhibitedly than was her wont.

She became aware suddenly of where the front-row forward's bleery eyes were focused.

"You got a *re*-markable pair of lungs there, girlie," he remarked. "Let's go upstairs, you and me."

"Nope," Sue said.

"What-cher mean, nope?"

"Just nope."

"Gotta have a better reason than that."

"I'm bad at stairs."

"Then I'll carry you," the front-row forward said and grabbed her.

Sue felt one of her non-placid moments coming on. She took the man's nose between the knuckles of her first and second fingers and gave it a really hearty tweak. At the same time she remarked, "Take your paws off me, you big ape."

"Christ!" the forward said in honest disbelief. This was not the way chicks were supposed to react at parties.

His expression became really mean and unpleasant. Sue wasn't easily frightened but she began to feel a little uneasy. The man was lifting her off her feet and slinging her over his shoulder and his hands were getting their moneysworth. She thumped him with her fists but it was like thumping a bag of cement. No one seemed to be paying any attention. Then she heard Max's voice.

"Put her down, please."

The man put her down and stared at Max.

"Who the bloody hell are you?"

26

" Just a friend."

" Get stuffed friend," the forward said.

He had evidently decided it was a false alarm and was preparing to pick Sue up again.

Max, who seemed to be hardly drunk at all, hit him twice, first on the chin and then in the stomach. To Sue's surprise the big man went down—just like a bag of cement. He made no sign of getting up again. Now people were taking notice. Half a dozen stalwarts, the official chuckers-out, advanced in a phalanx. They grabbed Max by the seat of his trousers and the back of his collar and moved towards the door in an unstoppable bum-rush. As he passed, face downwards now and horizontal, Max remarked quite casually to her, " See you outside."

" I'll bring the coats." Sue called after him.

She had a job finding them but eventually managed it. She put on her own and, carrying Max's, made her way back along the hall to the front door. It was open and clouds of tobacco smoke and the fumes of the hip-bath were escaping through it and befouling the night air outside. The chuckers-out were dusting their hands. They let her pass and as she went down the steps she heard the door slam behind her. Max was picking himself up from the pavement. He grinned at her in the light of a street lamp. She grinned back and helped him on with his coat.

" Sorry to take you from your black girl—she looked pretty," Sue said.

" Oh that's all right, we'd finished our business. Well, it wasn't a bad party, was it?"

" It put in the evening," Sue said.

Max looked up and down the deserted street.

" I'll stand you a taxi if we can find one—"

" No—let's walk."

" You really want to?" he asked. " It's miles and bloody miles."

" I really want to."

" Come on then."

Then arms around each other they strolled off towards Roxton Gate. They kept in step, Sue taking rather longer strides than usual and Max rather shorter. High over London the moon seemed to be keeping pace with them. After a while they began to sing songs from the charts, quietly, so as not to disturb the sleeping houses.

TWO

THE BOUTIQUE was not far from Carnaby Street and was owned by a Jew who lived over the shop. He was a middle-aged ex-boxer who had once been welterweight champion of the Southern Area or some such title. Sue and Piggy seldom saw him except when he came to collect the takings and lodge them at the nearby bank, but he was always at hand in case of need. Even when he had to go out, the girl who acted as housekeeper (it seemed to be a different one every week) always knew where he was and could fetch him in a couple of minutes. He was a widower but whether by death or mutual agreement—or disagreement—was never made clear.

After the first week or two he had decided that the two girls were trustworthy and left them to it. It was his policy to give good value and be content with a small percentage profit on a big turnover and he had a loyal clientele, mostly working-class. His face was like a squashed cheese and his nose was spread all over it, hardly standing out at all, as a result of ring battles long ago. Both Sue and Piggy liked him very much. He paid them generously and called them his young ladies.

29

They called him 'Uncle Ikey' behind his back but Mr. Rottger to his flattened face.

Sue and Piggy were the only members of the *kibbutz* who had known each other slightly before its inception. Piggy was undoubtedly the plainest of the four girls and was very conscious of the fact, although men generally found her attractive (certainly Willie Torr, with whom she was room-sharing since the last change-round, had made no complaint). So really both girls had the beginnings of an inferiority complex niggling at them, Sue about her bust measurement and Piggy about her plain face—not, mind you, that it was actually what most people would call plain. It was, as a matter of fact, an extremely pleasant face, it just didn't quite measure up to the unusually high standard of the other three girls. Each knew about the other's worry and would often try to counteract it, without realising that the other was doing the very same thing. For instance, Piggy might say, "My God, have you been dieting?—you're going away to nothing. You want to watch it, Sue, you do honestly." Or Sue might remark casually, "When you turned your head there you looked the spit of Raquel Welch. Hasn't any one else ever noticed it?—they must, really." That sort of thing.

The boutique opened at ten. On fine mornings Sue and Piggy usually walked the mile from Roxton Gate. On wet ones they took the underground, getting off at Oxford Circus, but that still left them a quarter of a mile from the boutique. The great advantage of working there was that you got first chance to buy any attractive new line that came in. They passed this benefit on to the other members of the *kibbutz*, who became regular customers, particularly Olga and Denise. They all paid the usual prices without any fiddling, because they knew Mr. Rottger pared his profit to the economic minimum; anyway, fiddling wouldn't have been easy even had they wanted to, for Mr. Rottger was no fool. He only gave his trust when he felt sure it wouldn't be abused. Even then you couldn't have fooled him for long.

This morning was fine so Sue and Piggy were walking to the boutique. Sue had had a slight headache on waking as a result of the hip-bath concoction but Max had given her some sort of fizzing cure that had helped, and the rest of the headache had disappeared completely when she got into the spring air.

" You were at a party last night with Max, weren't you?" Piggy remarked as they turned into Poland Street. " How did it go?"

Sue giggled.

" I nearly got raped."

" What's wrong with that?" Piggy asked jocularly.

" Only that it was an ape, not a man. Max knocked him out."

" Heavens—no one ever knocked anyone out over me."

" Any of them would. Don't try to kid me you don't attract men. How's Willie?"

" Oh Willie's fine. He doesn't normally go around knocking people out but he's in good working shape. Except that he can't get a plot. You remember the last one?"

" About the pop singer? I thought it stank."

" Me too. Only I hadn't the guts to tell him. Olga did, though."

" Good for Olga."

" You know, Willie *can* write—if only he'd something to write about."

" It's the *kibbutz*'s secret sorrow," Sue said. " We really must all sit down and try to think up a plot for Willie. If we all spent half an hour a day on it something might happen—"

" No, it wouldn't work. Willie says you can't handle someone else's plot. It's got to be your own." Piggy suddenly sounded depressed. " Maybe it's time for another change-round of room-mates. It might inspire him."

" It didn't before. We've wrung all the changes at least once. No matter who he was with Willie would still have trouble with his plots."

" Poor Willie," Piggy sighed. " What *can* we do for him?"

" Just give him plenty of lovin'," Sue said.

They arrived at the boutique, rang the bell at the house door four times quickly as a signal, then went round to the front of the shop. It was opened by a girl they hadn't seen before. This one was Jewish looking and younger than the usual run, with lots of curves, a turned-up nose and a cheeky, sexy face. It was also a pleasant face, with merry eyes.

" You'll be the young ladies?" she asked.

" It's a matter of opinion." Piggy said, " but that's what Mr. Rottger calls us."

" I'm Rebby, the new housekeeper," the girl said. " Rebecca, really. It's Miss Bottome and Miss Farthingale, isn't it?"

" That's right—I'm Sue Bottome," Sue said. " Welcome to the boutique, Rebby."

They all shook hands and the girl said, " Pleased to

meet you, I'm sure. Mr. Rottger may keep to his bed today on account of having had a disturbed night. But I was to take any messages."

"There's nothing at the moment I can think of, Rebby," Sue said.

"If anything turns up, we'll let you know," Piggy added. "In the meantime, look after him, Rebby."

"Oh, I'm doing that, Miss Farthingale," Rebby said enthusiastically. "He's ever so nice, isn't he?—not good looking or anything, but nice."

"We think so too," Piggy said.

Rebby went back up the stairs to the flat above. They watched her go. She wore a mini skirt, black net stockings (not tights because they could see her suspenders) and had a distinct wiggle.

"I like this one," Piggy remarked.

"He should have a lot of fun, bless him," Sue said. "May his nights all be disturbed."

"Amen," Piggy intoned. She had put her fingers together and was looking over an imaginary pair of spectacles.

It turned out to be quite a busy day at the boutique but otherwise uneventful. Each girl took a break for a snack lunch in the staff-room at the back and managed a cup of tea morning and afternoon, while the other held the fort.

Rebecca prepared the snack lunches but Sue and Piggy made their own cups of tea as and when they could spare the time. Mr. Rottger did not appear at all that day.

As they were walking back to Roxton Gate that evening through the crowded street, Piggy said, "We've got to do something about it, Sue."

" What—Uncle Ikey?"

" No—Willie's plots."

Sue didn't reply at once. Then she said, " You're not falling in love with Willie by any chance, are you, Piggy?"

" Me?—great heavens, no," Piggy replied quickly. " I'm just sorry for him."

" Honest to God—?"

" Honest to God."

" That's all right, then," Sue said with relief.

The ardent *kibbutzer* in Sue was always ready to spring to the defence of their communal way of living. To Sue the continuance of the *kibbutz* was her only guarantee of freedom from the conventions of her parents, who were Bible-thumpers. Some of these conventions seemed so palpably absurd to Sue that she had taken a sickener against them all. The most absurd now seemed to be the one which taught that men and women (but particularly women) should confine their lovemaking to a single partner. This seemed to Sue not only unnatural but positively evil. To fall in love with one person exclusively was to be possessive and therefore selfish. How much more sensible to use sex as it was obviously intended to be used. Only when there was an absence of attraction should its solace be withheld. The *kibbutz* afforded reasonable variety of partner and, since the members were hand-picked, ensured mutual attraction. If any complications arose, as well they might—well, these could best be ironed out by the members themselves in co-operation.

She knew a lot of other girls were enjoying this new freedom in circumstances not very dissimilar to the Roxton *kibbutz*. For them marriage was no longer the high-

34

watermark of female achievement, the crowning snatch that called for all the circus celebrations. The age-old battlecry of the hunting mother—far better an unhappy marriage for my daughter than that she should suffer the disgrace of being left on the shelf—had no meaning now.

Sue was perfectly aware that her Bible-thumping parents, had they known all the details, would undoubtedly have called the *kibbutz* a disorderly house. That was just funny. There simply couldn't be a more orderly house than the *kibbutz*.

Now, walking back from the boutique, Sue had feared for a moment that Piggy might be in danger of forgetting the ideals of the *kibbutz*. Only betrayal from within, Sue felt, could destroy it. But Piggy's quick denial had reassured her.

Olga Beloff lay with her hands behind her head and watched Ted Allard trim his beard in the mirror above the wash-basin. It wasn't her week to make the breakfast so she could afford this luxury. On her duty week she had to rise before Ted and then it was he who lay on and watched her dressing.

She loved watching Ted do his topiary act. Sometimes she almost expected his beard to take the shape of a fox or a peacock or a hen sitting on its nest, just as bushes and hedges took shape under the shears. She particularly liked the way he pulled his face about with his left hand —the male equivalent of a female's mouthings when she put on lipstick, Olga supposed.

" You've left a wiggly bit," she said helpfully.

" Where?" Ted asked out of the side of his mouth without halting the razor.

" Left side below chin."

35

" Dope—I haven't come to that yet."

Ted finished shaving, dabbed at his face with the blue towel—the pink was hers—and put on his shirt. As he was buttoning it he came over beside the bed and looked down at her. They screwed up their noses at each other. Olga pulled her flaxen hair over her face, then parted it like a shy little girl peeping through a curtain. Ted bent and kissed her on the mouth, at the same time slipping his hand under the bedclothes and rubbing her bare tummy playfully—she was only wearing her pyjama top.

" Time to get up," Ted said. " None of your Russian layabout tricks here. Rotten bad example for the English working classes."

" You smell of shaving cream."

" And you of the pine forests of the Ukraine."

" Come off it," Olga said, laughing.

" Thanks for a good night—now have a good day, little playmate. But don't let anyone else pat your tummy."

" Go away," Olga said. " And take your hand with you."

He gave her tummy a last pat, put on his tie and jacket and went whistling out of the bedroom.

Olga stretched herself and lay for a moment longer thinking about the different morning-techniques of the four men. Ted was cheeky and occasionally serious, Tubby boisterous and full of himself, Willie gentle, Max off-hand—but all in their own way considerate. We're lucky with our male *kibbutzers*, she thought. She wondered suddenly if there could ever be a really mean, spiteful argument in the *kibbutz*, with hurtful words hurled around. She found it hard to imagine.

She got up and had a quick shower, put on her clothes

and face and made the bed, all in about ten minutes.
But she was still last down to breakfast.

All seven, already seated, thumped the table and
shouted at her in unison, " Russian layabout!—Russian
layabout!"

" The English pig-dog Allard—the one with the beard
—has put you up to it," Olga told them in a deep foreign
voice. " Simpletons that you are, you have allowed yourselves to be brainwashed—pigs, pigs, *bourgeois* pigs all
of you."

But the pigs made room for her and she sat down
happily among them.

They chattered their way through breakfast, each rising
and going about his or her business as they finished.
Each of the men kissed any or all of the girls on his
way out, as fancy moved him. Tubby, as usual, was the
first away because of his habit of gobbling his food. It
didn't seem to do his innards any harm for his pink
cheery face was always the picture of health beneath
his mop of curly ginger hair. " Don't take any wooden
nickels, children," he said as he left the table.

Then Ted Allard departed to look after the lights at
one of the B.B.C. studios where a play was in rehearsal.
On his heels Denise left for the store in Oxford Street,
and Sue and Piggy for their boutique—they had some
hanging of newly arrived stock to do before opening.

Max went after consulting his notebook to check on
that day's calls. Max was the only one who had a car,
an ancient MG which he kept in the mews at the back.
At first he had offered lifts to any of the others going his
way, but his car was always so jampacked with boxes
of typewriter ribbons and other stationery samples that
it was about as comfortable as a bed of nails, so his

passengers had defected one by one. Denise even swore her bottom was so permanently and deeply scarred it would show through her slacks and in future no one would line up at the store window to admire it. She was, she said, seriously considering sueing Max for loss of amenity. Every morning when Max went round to the mews he expected to find the car pinched, not for its own sake but because of the samples inside. But it still survived, sitting there like an aged down-and-out who has spent a night on a park bench.

This morning Olga (whom all the men seemed never to miss a chance of kissing) was the last to go except for Willie, who would wash up the breakfast things before Mrs. Williams arrived. Mrs. Williams had enough to do just keeping the house clean, and Willie got off other duties on account of this morning chore. Olga paused to touch the top of Willie's head on her way out.

"Hope the muse works today," she said. "'Bye now, Willie."

Willie grunted.

"Thanks—but my bloody muse is a lazy good-for-nothing slut, all promises but no performance."

"Try taking her to the British Museum—Conrad or someone used to get the germ of his plots there—"

"Hey, that's not a bad idea—I just might," Willie said, brightening. "You've forgotten something—you're not just getting away with a lousy pat on the head."

"Oh, you," Olga said.

But she came back and gave him a quick kiss on the forehead. He made a sound like a purring cat. "'Bye now, Olga—don't sit on the boss's knee."

Olga fought her way on to the Metropolitan line and had to stand right through to the City (an offered knee would go well now, she thought). The firm of Sloane, Medway & Sloane, Solicitors, was in Moorgate. Olga worked for the middle partner, Mr. Medway. He was fortyish, very Guards and City and so far she had found him the most correct of bosses and the soul of probity. His idea of excess seemed to be to take an afternoon off for golf every now and then, but not oftener than once a month. (Not, she knew with a woman's intuition, that he was always as unaware of her presence as he pretended to be.)

Every morning after going through his mail he called her in. This morning while waiting for his summons Olga opened her compact and stared at her face in the little mirror for a moment. She thought, I'm a lucky girl. I've had a happy childhood and now my private love-life is satisfying and varied and my business life is uncomplicated and well enough paid to ensure independence and make my private life possible. It will go on this way as far as I can see into the future. Only when I become old will I have to make other arrangements. But that is a long, long way ahead. In the meantime life will continue to be fun, as it was meant to be. I will be nice to people and hope that they will be nice to me in return, because that too is the way life was meant to be.

The inter-office unit buzzed. She flicked the switch over and Mr. Medway's voice said (just as it always did), "Good morning, Miss Beloff, will you come in please?"

She picked up her notebook and pencil and went through to his office. He glanced up at her briefly from behind his desk and gave a barely perceptible bob of the head. She did not know it but he was sitting and feeling just as he had sat and felt during his years as

Adjutant in the Guards Depot. His greying hair was precisely of the same shortness back and sides as it had been then and his little military moustache was like something painted on his upper lip. Olga sat down opposite him and waited, being careful not to show too much leg. Anytime she was careless about that Mr. Medway, without looking directly at it, would cough and she would tuck her skirt more closely round her.

She knew exactly what was coming. This was security —the blessed business security that made her private happiness possible. She knew that in ten seconds precisely Mr. Medway would say, "Take a letter please, Miss Beloff."

Ten seconds later he said, "Take a letter please, Miss Beloff."

Mrs. Williams let herself into 32 Roxton Gate. Usually that young Mr. Torr was sitting typing somewhere, but this morning the house was empty (Willie had, as a matter of fact, taken Olga's advice and gone to the British Museum).

Mrs. Williams made herself a cup of tea. She didn't spend unduly long over it, however, for she was a conscientious woman. Then she went quickly through the bedrooms just to see that everything was ship-shape. All the beds had been made—the young people were very good about that. She emptied a few ashtrays and cleared out the laundry baskets. It always amused her to find lace panties and jockey shorts in the same basket. The carpet in one of the bedrooms—Miss Beloff's—didn't look as if it had been vacuumed lately, so she did that. Then she vacuumed the stairs and landings and hall, and dusted and polished where necessary.

The dishes, as usual, were all washed and put away, but the dishcloths looked as if they could do with a boil. So she boiled them and spun them dry and hung them up.

Usually she made up the bundle and list for the laundry and dropped them in at the laundry office on her way home. But today she seemed to have a bit of time on hand, so she washed the gentlemen's shirts and the ladies' blouses—those were the things she liked doing—spun and ironed those that required ironing and left them in neat bundles for their owners to claim when they came home. The rest of the laundry—for she couldn't of course, do it all—she bundled into two bolster cases. Because of the bit of washing she had done herself she would only have to make one trip to the laundry office today, a bolster under each arm; quite often she had to make two or three, but that never worried her for the office was only round the corner.

As she put on her hat in the hall, Mrs. Williams, who was a widow and lived by herself, felt a twinge of envy. That was the only drawback about 'doing' 32—it made her *that* nostalgic. In her youth, before her marriage, nobody had been fonder of a bit of nookie than herself (when she got it legally and more regularly with Mr. Williams after marriage, it somehow didn't seem quite so good). Only in those pre-marriage romps you had to be bloody careful; and no matter how careful you were you ran a big risk of getting caught. Nowadays with these pills and things it must be a cakewalk. You could settle back and enjoy yourself without the niggling fear of consequences breaking your concentration just as you came to the boil.

Such pleasures, churched or unchurched, were now,

B*   41

worse luck, only a distant if evergreen memory. Mrs. Williams suddenly chuckled wistfully as she remembered the story about the old lady whose regular doctor had retired. When the new one came he found the old lady in bed and in order to learn something of her case history enquired if she had ever been bedridden. To which the old lady had replied, with a gleam in her eye, " Aye, I got my share—those were the days, doctor, those were the days."

Mrs. Williams had a last look round the hall, feeling very akin to the old lady. She peeped in the mirror and looked hurriedly away—the resemblance to Margaret Rutherford was more marked than ever. Jealousy gets you nowhere, she thought. So good luck to everyone in 32, I say—they're making the most of it while the going's good. They'll be swapping and doing it fancy and all the rest of it, more power to them—maybe even now and again having one of them orgies. Mrs. Williams grew poetic. " Gather ye rosebuds while ye may," she said aloud to the newel-post, which had suddenly assumed a phallic symbolism, " 'cos they don't last for ever."

All the way to the laundry office she kept thinking, those were the days—those were the days . . .

Piggy Farthingale usually made a trip south of the river once a week to visit her parents. They lived over a pub—The Blue Hound—in Wortley Street not far from the Old Vic.

Mr. Farthingale had been a Flying Officer in Hitler's war and with his gratuity had bought the pub and married the barmaid who went with it. It was an unlikely environment and alliance for Fred Farthingale, who had been One of the Few. Now, verging on fifty, he still kept his handlebars moustache and some vestige of his good looks, though there was an increasingly Rubens-esque floridness about his wattles.

Piggy usually went straight from the boutique every Tuesday evening and stayed for tea at The Blue Hound, leaving as soon as she could decently get away afterwards. She always walked from the Waterloo underground to Wortley Street with the apprehension of a matador going into the bullring and wondering what the bulls would be like today; walking back afterwards she shared the matador's thankfulness that the fight was over and there had been no actual physical goring. It isn't a very good analogy because the matador does it for money and acclaim whereas Piggy did it solely out of a sense of duty.

Her mother had been christened Victoria but everyone, including the customers in the 'public', called her Vicky. She was still a blonde and still pretty in a sexy, brassy sort of way. It irked both parents that their daughter didn't measure up to their own standard of good looks.

This Tuesday was no different from all the others. Piggy went in by the house-door and climbed the lino-covered stairs to the first-floor-back behind the pub. In the living room, with its faded red and gold Empire wall-paper, the table was set for tea. Fred Farthingale was already seated at it, as she knew he would be, a bottle of whisky beside his plate and a half empty glass in his hand. He probably drank a bottle a day nowadays, Piggy calculated, which must make an appreciable dent in his profits. The smell of bacon and eggs frying came from the kitchen—Vicky's culinary vision never carried beyond bacon and eggs for tea on Tuesdays.

Piggy went over and kissed her father on the forehead. "Hello, Fred," she said, "how are things going?"

"Christ, if it isn't Peg," he said. He spoke as if taken by surprise but Piggy knew he was expecting her. He called towards the kitchen, "Hey, Vicky—it's our own plain wholesome little daughter Peg—"

"Be in in a minute—can't leave the pan," Vicky shouted back. "Keep her entertained with your charming conversation in the meantime—"

"Sit down and have a snifter, Peg," Fred said.

"Well, I don't know—"

"Oh for God's sake," her father said. He took a tea-cup from the table, poured a little whisky into it and pushed it towards her. "Good for virgins—you are a virgin, aren't you?"

"Does it really matter?" Piggy asked.

"Not a fart, m'dear—just making conversation."

"How's—how's business, Fred?" Piggy asked.

"During the day, so-so. But it bucks up no end at night when your mother serves in the bar. You know why—?"

"Yes, I know why," Piggy said, but she knew she'd have to listen to it again. She took a sip of the whisky. She didn't like neat whisky but to go into the kitchen to top it up with water would only make him worse.

"'Cos she wears a low neck," her father went on, speaking loudly so that his voice would carry to the kitchen. "It doesn't matter a fart what quality of booze you're selling if you've got a barmaid with a low neck and big boobs. You should see the customers crowding the counter to get an eyeful when she pulls the bottles. The ones at the back climb on the shoulders of those in front. Your mother may have her faults—in fact, she *has* her faults, about two million of them—but her boobs

44

aren't one of them." He cackled with relish, his handle-bars moustache wobbling. "Size, shape, bounce—you name it, your mother's got it right there inside her blouse. Somewhere in there too she's got the heart of a stripper."

For a moment Piggy thought of Sue and how every-one in the *kibbutz* kept telling her how thin she was, just to ease her selfconsciousness about her bust measure-ment. For the thousandth time Piggy asked herself, why do I come? But she didn't really need to ask. She came because her father was the saddest person she knew. He had once been brave and kind; even as recently as fourteen or fifteen years ago, when she had been a very small girl and he had been in his middle thirties, he had seemed to her a charmer—an erratic charmer, per-haps, but still a charmer. Yet even then he must have been spiralling down like Icarus. How had it happened? Probably a combination of things—The Blue Hound, Vicky, some fatal flaw of character in himself. But mostly the flaw in himself. Maybe when you'd once shot down twenty-two Messerschmitts the only thing left to shoot down was yourself. For an hour in the week Piggy could stand it but that was the limit.

"How's that Jew man?" her father asked.

"Mr. Rottger?—oh he's fine."

"Watch him, m'dear. These Jews are like the buses —on top of you before you know."

"He's kind," Piggy said quietly.

"Don't let those big-nosed circumcised bastards fool you—don't be a Gentile sucker." He cackled again. "Their big noses you can see but you don't know about the other till it's too late."

Vicky came in from the kitchen with a tray on which

45

was a teapot and three plates of bacon and eggs and fried bread. She greeted her daughter and sat down and poured the tea. They were, Piggy told herself, three as ill-assorted people as you could find in the whole of London. And yet, in some queer way, her mother, though less outrageous than her father, was the odd one out.

" What have you been doing with yourself, Peg?" Vicky asked.

" Oh, just the usual things," Piggy said. " You know—work, eat, sleep."

Her mother was inspecting her critically. Vicky's eyes were shaded with a turquoise tint, she had on false lashes and unquestionably she was, for her age, a fine big buxom sexy woman. Take twenty years off her and it wasn't hard to understand why Flying Officer Fred Farthingale, fresh from the barren graveyard in the sky, had fallen for her. Even Piggy could see that.

" You want to try a different shade of lipstick, dearie —something with more colour in it," Vicky said. " The one you've got on does nothing for you, nothing at all."

" I've tried them all," Piggy said.

" For Christ's sake leave the girl alone," Fred shouted suddenly.

Vicky said calmly, conversationally, " Of course you'd know about leaving people alone, wouldn't you, Fred? At least I was talking about her mouth, not her boobs. Why don't you just pour another glass of whisky into you and shut up?" She turned back to her daughter. " How's the girl you work with?—Sue something, isn't it?"

" Sue Bottome—oh, she's fine," Piggy said.

" If she wants to keep fine, tell her to watch that Jew bastard," Fred mumbled.

46

" Why don't you bring her along sometimes for bacon and eggs?" Vicky said.

" There she goes, playing Mummy the Bacon-and-Egg Queen," her husband cackled. " Jesus, who does she think she's fooling?" He seemed to be talking to himself now.

" Maybe I will," Piggy said.

" You're not ashamed of us, are you?" her mother asked.

" No, of course not, Vicky."

Piggy was thinking, it's not like talking to your mother at all, it's like talking to a stranger.

" Of course she's ashamed of us," Fred cut in thickly. " She's not a bloody half-wit."

" Give your father a couple of minutes longer and he'll doze off in a stupor with his mouth hanging open," Vicky said evenly to Piggy. " Then we can have our chat in peace—"

" Chat?" Fred said. He cackled again. " *Chat?* What in Christ's name could you two chat about? You've nothing in common. Peg mayn't be a beauty queen but at least she's a Farthingale. You're only a barmaid with big boobs."

" You'll notice your father retains all the Farthingale charm," Vicky said. " It may be the least bit phoney now but it's still there—"

" Who's phoney?" Fred demanded. He leaned across the table towards Piggy, his forefinger at the side of his nose, and winked at her. " Tell you something you may now know, Peg—underneath that peroxide muck your mother's as grey as a bloody old cow badger—"

" Oh go shoot down a Messerschmitt," Vicky said contemptuously.

That was how it went on for the next half-hour, pointless, childish, each continuing the process of destroying the other. But it was Fred, Piggy knew, whose destruction would be accomplished first; Vicky was tougher, less vulnerable—and she didn't drink. During that half-hour Fred never quite dozed off, though his head kept nodding. As Piggy was leaving he looked at her apparently quite soberly and said in a low earnest voice, " I'll be in better form next time—you *will* come back next week, won't you, Peg? No matter how bloody awful it is for you, say you'll come back."

He was like a sad small boy pleading now. Piggy didn't try to rationalise his conduct, she just accepted that here were two people whose marriage had been a disaster and who now hated each other. There was nothing she herself could do—during her visits she hardly ever spoke more than a dozen sentences, none of them of any consequence. Yet her visits were important to her father. Somehow that made a sort of sense.

" Yes," she promised, " I'll come back."

" I don't know how you do it, dearie," Vicky said. " Honest to God I don't."

Piggy kissed her father and mother then and said, " Be nice to each other. 'Bye, now."

What sort of bondage was it, she wondered, that kept them together? Oddly, as she was leaving, they nearly always stopped snapping at each other for about a minute. That was another thing she could never understand. Yet perhaps it was that more than anything else that brought her back.

As she went down the stairs into Wortley Street she thought about the *kibbutz*. It was lovely just to think of a place where people were kind and considerate to each other.

48

Tubby Weatherstone was probably the least responsible member of the Roxton *kibbutz*. He was chock-full of good intentions and resolutions but was not difficult to waylay, particularly if the waylayer had a feminine configuration.

There were four milk bars in the chain that employed him, all within a short-walk radius of the Strand. The main one was in the Strand itself and the other three were respectively in Maiden Lane, Henrietta Street and the near end of Aldwych. They were owned by a small syndicate headed by Mr. Kaladopoulos, who was managing director, the others being sleeping partners. All four branches gave the usual soda fountain service and snacks such as hot-dogs and steakburgers but no very complicated meals.

Tubby's official designation was junior personnel officer but the word junior was really a bit of bluff since there was only one personnel officer. Really he acted as link-man between the four establishments. He dropped into each at varying times of the day, walked through the kitchens and chatted to the managers, dealt with any staff problems, shunted waitresses as necessary between the branches and in general kept his finger on the pulse of the complex and reported the rate of heart-beat to Mr. Kaladopoulos.

It was a strict rule of the syndicate that the male officers should not date the waitresses. This preserved the authority of the hierarchy; the punishment for breach of this rule was the instant sacking of the male. The female, as the subordinate, was regarded as a non-offender (also, a glamorous waitress who attracted her male superiors could also presumably attract customers, which was the opposite of an offence). Knowing this, Tubby had steeled himself to march straight up to the office without looking right or left at the female staff. So, except for those few who had asked for an interview about some personal problem, he knew only half a dozen or so of them by sight.

Tubby's job was not a particularly onerous one, but it performed a necessary function in the complex and required a quick eye for possible irregularities and a general resourcefulness, both of which Tubby possessed. What he didn't possess was the ability to hold down a job for long, although it must also be said that he never had any difficulty in finding another one. The present post suited him, however, and he had made up his mind that this time it would be different.

The Strand place was Tubby's base (as it also was Mr. Kaladopoulos's) and his first task each morning was to ring round the three branches and find out from their managers if they had any problems such as staff shortages, misdemeanours or complaints. By the time he had finished these calls, Mr. Kaladopoulos would have arrived and Tubby would make a short verbal report to him. Between them they would then decide what action was called for. Thereafter Tubby's function boiled down to taking the agreed action, keeping an eye on the managers and generally seeing that the branches ran efficiently.

On this particular morning the only problem raised was by the Henrietta Street manager, one of whose waitresses had not clocked in. It was a run-of-the-mill occurrence which Tubby usually solved by ringing up the agency and getting them to send round the most suitable girl available. But this morning Mr. Kaladopoulos was in one of his moods of retrenchment, which came on him periodically like bouts of malaria. When Tubby made his report and suggested contacting the agency, Mr. Kaladopoulos, who was a small bald man, threw up his hands and made a grimace.

"The agency, the agency!—of the agency I am sick. Agencies charge fees—this we forget, yes? But now we will do different. From one of the other branches a girl you will borrow and send her to Henrietta Street—so it is solved"—he snapped his fingers—"like that, yes?"

"No," Tubby said patiently. "We've tried that often before and none of the other managers can ever spare a girl. In any case it would only be robbing Peter to pay Paul—"

"Who are these men, please?" Mr. Kaladopoulos asked suspiciously. "We have staff I do not know about, yes—?"

"No," Tubby said again. "It's just a saying—it means we'd only be switching the shortage from one branch to another—"

"This is—how you say it?—the big load of codswallop," Mr. Kaladopoulos said. "Of course managers will make pretence they cannot spare staff—they do not want to spoil the job, yes? But I tell you, one there always is who can spare a member of staff more better than the others. Go now and find out for yourself which manager is making the codswallop—maybe it may even be the Henrietta Street one. Talk to them nice—humour them, yes—but do not give in to them. The telephone is not good for humouring—go round by your feet. This is what we pay you for. And in future think last to call the agency, not first as now. What you say?"

"All right—I'll go round by my feet," Tubby said.

He set off round the branches and found that the

Henrietta Street manager's problem was genuine—certainly during the two hours from twelve to two he would need another girl. So Tubby visited the other two branches and decided, after much discussion, that the Maiden Lane one could just, at a pinch, spare one of its waitresses for these two hours. But the manager made a poor face and Tubby had to exert his powers of persuasion to the utmost.

"Look," he said, "I don't expect you to send your star girl—just someone with arms and legs to fill a gap for a couple of hours."

"That'll be Miss Hicks," the manager said pessimistically. "She doesn't like being mucked about—it'll mean a proper set-to—you know what they are nowadays—"

"All right, send her up to me and I'll have a word with her," Tubby offered rashly.

They had been talking in the office upstairs. When the girl came up, Tubby found himself blinking suddenly. It came as a surprise that the Kaladopoulos syndicate, without his knowledge, had such talent on its staff. Miss Hicks was a dolly, a poppet, a real demolisher of good resolutions. On her the lemon coloured uniform looked like a Dior creation.

He found himself asking, "What's your first name, Miss Hicks?"

"It's Mitzi, Mr. Weatherstone," Miss Hicks said, fluttering her eyelashes at him.

"Oh—so you know me—?"

"All of us girls know *you*, Mr. Weatherstone. We see you come in though you never notice us."

Five minutes later Mitzi had agreed to fill in at Henrietta Street for the two hours of the lunch-time rush.

She had also, after a very slight token hesitation, agreed to go out with Tubby for an evening meal and afterwards to the pictures.

They met after hours at a quiet restaurant off Leicester Square. Mitzi didn't sparkle conversationally during the meal but she was exciting to look at across the table. Later they went to the Odeon and were lucky to get a back seat in the balcony. This was more Mitzi's line of country. She proved co-operative and gave promise of being even more so.

When the lights went up at the end of the last showing and they rose to go, from the seat immediately in front of them there also rose a small bald man, who turned and stared at Tubby and Mitzi.

" Your voice I thought it was, though you did not make much talk," Mr. Kaladopoulos said.

" Good picture, wasn't it?" Tubby remarked. He could not think of anything else to say. He hoped Mr. Kaladopoulos might not recognise Mitzi as a member of his staff but immediately realised from the look in his eye that he had.

" Not bloody much of the picture you saw," Mr. Kaladopoulos said. " The rules you know. Do not trouble tomorrow to come in. No more do you work there any longer—ever."

" If you'd let me phone instead of sending me round by my feet this wouldn't have happened," Tubby protested in an aggrieved voice.

" Do not give me big load of codswallop," Mr. Kaladopoulos said. He nodded to the woman at his side, presumably Mrs. Kaladopoulos. " Come, Anna, let us go into the fresh air. There is a stuffiness here."

Tubby saw Mitzi to the street door of her digs.

"I'm sorry you lost your job over me, Tubby," she said.

"Are you going to make it up to me—?"

"I'm sure I don't know what you mean," Mitzi said. "But you can come up for a cup of tea if you promise to be quiet."

"As a mouse," Tubby said, grinning.

She let herself in and switched on a light in the hall. "It's only a bed-sitter," she said. He followed her shapely legs up the stairs, his heart thumping.

Something more than an hour later as he came down them, he thought, why do I do this? It's not as if I didn't get sex—good sex, the best—at the *kibbutz*. I really must stop chasing dollies . . .

Two days later he found another job—as manager to a chain of launderettes.

THREE

On the following Sunday afternoon Piggy was alone in the *kibbutz*. All the others had gone out—the girls with Max in his car which he had cleared of samples for the occasion, and the three men to play billiards at a club. Piggy had stayed in because there was a travel documentary she wanted to see on the television.

She watched it through with interest and had just switched off when the door-bell rang. She answered it and found a pleasant-faced old gentleman with white side-whiskers on the step.

He asked if Willie Torr was in and Piggy said she was sorry but there was no one in except herself and could she take a message?

The old gentleman studied her face carefully—not in a frightening way for he was a most un-frightening person—and then said, "Not a message, I think. But could we have a chat? That might be even better than if I saw Willie himself. You see, I'm his uncle—on the paternal side."

"Come in, Mr. Torr," Piggy said, wondering what Willie's uncle could possibly find to talk to her about.

She took him into the sitting-room and unearthed

a bottle of sherry and poured a glass for him and one for herself. She felt she could do no less for Willie's uncle.

He sipped it appreciatively and asked, " May I know your name?"

" I'm Piggy Farthingale," she told him. " Please call me Piggy."

" Peggy?"

" No, Piggy."

He looked startled for a moment, then gave a little old-fashioned bow of acknowledgement and said, " Well, Piggy, don't be offended if I ask you another rather personal question. Are you by any chance Willie's girl?"

Piggy smiled at that. " No," she said, " I'm afraid I'm not."

" Humph. But, I take it, you know him well?"

Piggy suddenly found herself flushing slightly. It wasn't one of her habits and it annoyed her intensely that it should happen just at this point. Fortunately it didn't last long and it wasn't a very deep flush but she felt sure the old gentleman had noticed it, although he looked away and pretended he hadn't.

" Yes," she told him simply, " I know Willie pretty well." She felt quite positive that her flush had given away the fact that she and Willie were at present sleeping together.

" Humph," Mr. Torr said, looking back at her. " Then you'll probably also know that Willie's an orphan— his parents were killed in a plane crash some years ago. They weren't very well off and, being Willie's nearest relative, I thought it only right I should give him a small allowance. I'm a widower myself and can afford it, having no family of my own, so there was nothing very meritorious about the gesture." He paused and took another appreciative sip at the sherry. "I say, this is rather good stuff. Now tell me, Piggy—what do you think of Willie's efforts at writing?"

He had tossed off the question casually but Piggy had the feeling that he had decided her opinion was worth having and that her answer would somehow be important to him. So she thought very carefully before she replied.

"I think Willie has it in him to be a good writer—perhaps even a very good one. The trouble is he can't find a theme that suits him. Oh, he's made plenty of starts—but they've all been false ones. It's not inability to write, it's inability to find something worthwhile to write about."

"Humph," Willie's uncle said again. He finished his sherry thoughtfully. Piggy filled his glass again and took another half-glass herself. She had the feeling that Mr. Torr hadn't come from—wherever he'd come from, just to have an aimless chat. He didn't look like that kind of old gentleman to her. He hadn't said his punch-line yet.

"Some people," Mr. Torr remarked, "seem to work better when they're free from all economic anxiety. Others do their best work with the wolf scrabbling at the door—Schubert and chaps like that. Which category would you say Willie belongs to?"

What a question, Piggy thought. Oh lord, what a question. If I say honestly what I think, he'll probably cut off Willie's allowance. She felt a little prickle of anger somewhere inside her. Willie's uncle had no right to put her in such an invidious position. He knew nothing about her—nothing about her integrity or the value, if any, of her opinion. She could, of course, say that in her opinion Willie'd work better free of financial worry. But then she'd be telling a lie.

"That's hardly a fair question, is it, Mr. Torr?" she said. She said it quietly but she couldn't quite keep the annoyance out of her voice. She looked straight at him as she spoke and saw that he was looking even straighter at her.

"No, it isn't," he agreed. "Just the same, my dear, I'd like you to answer it."

Somewhere inside Piggy for just a moment the prickle of anger turned into an explosion. She didn't understand it—first she'd blushed and now she was exploding.

"Oh hell," she was horrified to hear herself say, "all right, if you *must* have my opinion, I think Willie's more likely to make it if the wolf keeps scrabbling at the door. I think—I'm not sure, mind you, but I think—he's the type that needs the pressure kept on. I also think I'm darned mean not to keep my big mouth shut—!"

She clapped her hand over her mouth immediately she had said it. Then she took her hand away and added, "I—I'm dreadfully sorry, Mr. Torr—I'm not usually so rude—"

He made a small gesture waving her apology aside and actually seemed to be trying not to smile.

"Humph," he said, "I knew your opinion would be an honest one. Let me make one thing clear, Piggy. My allowance to Willie is so small I consider the wolf is already at his door. I wasn't thinking of stopping it—it was something else altogether. You see, I own a house and a business and I'm also an old man who sometimes hears the swish of the scythe coming nearer. It's really

58

just a matter of timing. Willie'll get it in the end anyway. The question is, now or later?—which would be
best for Willie? You've helped me decide, my dear, and
I'm very grateful. We'll just let things jog along as they
are in the meantime."

Piggy stared at him.

" But my opinion may be quite wrong—"

" I'm aware of that—but where am I likely to get a
better one?" He took a card out of his pocket and handed
it to her; she noticed it had an address in Henley.
" Humph—keep that out of Willie's sight. And if you
change your opinion, let me know—just ring or, better
still, call. And now, Piggy, I must be going. Tell Willie
his Uncle Tim dropped in and was sorry to miss him—
just that and nothing more. Promise?"

" I promise," Piggy said dazedly.

" Not really true because as things turned out I'm
glad I missed him. I only meant to pump him about his
writing and try to decide for myself which type he was,
but talking to you has been much more illuminating.
Also, I don't know when I enjoyed a drop of sherry
more. Now, where did I leave my hat—?"

On the doorstep he paused and wagged a finger at her.

" Remember, Piggy, this is our secret. And if for
any reason you change your opinion, I'd be grateful if
you'd get in touch with me. Mark what I say, please
—for *any* reason, not just his writing. My only concern
is what's best for Willie. You understand?"

" I understand," Piggy said (about five per cent of it,
she added to herself).

For a moment longer he stood there, his eyes taking
in the visible parts of the house as if he could see through
them to the invisible parts beyond. Piggy suddenly had

59

the feeling that he was an uncommonly wise and understanding old bird. His eyes came back to her face and she caught a faint twinkle in them. "One last question," he said.

"Yes—?"

"Are there many young ladies like you around these days?"

"Lots and lots," she told him, laughing.

"Humph," he said, "then I think I was born too soon. A mere matter of fifty years or so."

It was such a nice compliment Piggy pecked him impulsively on the cheek; she did not doubt that in times long past many other lips had kissed that cheek. I've gone mad, she thought—this isn't me assaulting elderly gentlemen with my kisses—

"Humph—now I'm sure of it," he said.

Without another word he turned and went down the steps. As she went back into the house she thought, well, that's just about the most improbable interview I've ever had.

She simply didn't know what to make of Willie's uncle. An invitation to chase Willie and bring him to the altar? Hardly. In any case it wouldn't work, the *kibbutz* being anti-altar. She went upstairs and locked Uncle Tim's card away in her private drawer. She didn't really expect ever to have to refer to it. But in this world you never knew.

Mrs. Mont dropped in unexpectedly at the *kibbutz* one Thursday afternoon when only Mrs. Williams was there (mostly Mrs. Williams worked in the mornings but occasionally she switched to the afternoon).

She answered the door and said, "Yes?" to the slim,

distinguished-looking and somewhat 'county' lady on the doorstep.

"Is Miss Denise Mont in?" Mrs. Mont enquired.

"Oh, you'll never find any of 'em in at this time," Mrs. Williams said, "Except sometimes Mr. Torr—and even he's out at the moment. Can I take a message?"

"Well—not really," Mrs. Mont said. "I'm Denise's mother and I just wanted to see for myself how—er—things are."

"Oh—her mother," Mrs. Williams said. (Inwardly she added to herself, Oh Gawd!)

"Yes—I promised my daughter I'd drop in sometime when I was passing. Well, I happened to be passing this afternoon. Of course I should have let her know before-hand—but you know how one does things on the spur of the moment. Now that I'm here I might as well have a look around—don't you think?"

"I'm only the cleaner," Mrs. Williams said. (Spur of the moment my foot, she was thinking—the old faggot knew bloody well her daughter wouldn't be in on a Thursday afternoon).

"But that's splendid," Mrs. Mont said. "You'll know my daughter's room and everything."

Mrs. Williams was nonplussed. She couldn't very well turn Miss Denise's mother away. At the same time she would be letting down the members of the *kibbutz*—for whom Mrs. Williams had a very genuine affection—if she were to let Mrs. Mont nose around. From Mrs. Mont's appearance she judged that Denise's mother might not take quite the same view of life as Denise herself.

"Well, then, ma'am, you'd better come in, hadn't you?" she temporised.

"Thank you—just a quick peep at my daughter's room to make sure she's comfortable—"

"She's got all her comforts, ma'am. I can tell you that—"

"I'm sure she has—but you know what mothers are."

"Of course," Mrs. Williams said. She had been thinking very hard and very quickly. This was no time for panic. She showed Mrs. Mont not up the stairs but into the sitting-room. "But before I take you up, ma'am, you must let me make you a cup of tea—"

"No really—you musn't trouble—"

"Miss Denise would never forgive me if I let you away without a nice cup of tea," Mrs. Williams said with finality. "I won't be a jiffy."

"Very well, then—you're most kind," Mrs. Mont said, smiling.

Mrs. Williams found her a woman's magazine to anchor her and bustled out of the room. She hurried to the kitchen and put on the kettle. Then she climbed the stairs to Denise's room—Denise's and Tubby's—faster than she had ever climbed them before.

She didn't know Mrs. Mont's form—but she had all the appearance of a drawer-opener and a looker-under-pillows. Under Denise's pillow her baby-doll nightie was folded (Denise wasn't one of the pyjama brigade). Under the other pillow in the twin bed alongside, Tubby's aggressively masculine pyjamas made an unmistakable contrast. Mrs. Williams whisked the latter away. She also whisked away his shaving things which sat on the glass ledge beside the wash-basin, and his clothes and undergarments from the wardrobe and drawers. She didn't miss his slippers under the bed or the odds and ends lying about. Mrs. Williams really could move astonishingly fast in a worthy cause, even if it did make her breathless. She carted everything of Tubby's that she could find into the next bedroom, which happened to be Olga's and Ted's, and piled them up on the bed. Then she borrowed an armful of Olga's belongings and carried them into Denise's room. When she had arranged them as appropriately as she could, she cast a last critical eye round the room.

" Oh Gawd," she said.

In the shower cubicle she had noticed two towels hanging side by side on the chromium rail. One was embroidered with the word *Hers* and the other with the word *His*. So she grabbed them and ran back into Olga's room, where she managed to find a couple of plain ones to put in their places.

By now she could hear the kettle singing. So she tore downstairs and hurriedly put two cups and a plate of biscuits on a tray along with the teapot and cream and sugar and staggered with them to the sitting room.

" You don't mind if I have a cup along with you, do you, ma'am?" she asked, panting.

" Of course not," Mrs. Mont replied. Her voice sounded quite concerned because of Mrs. Williams's breathlessness. " But you shouldn't have rushed, really you shouldn't."

" No trouble at all," Mrs. Williams said. " Miss Denise would have been that upset if I'd let you go without a drop of tea."

They chatted together while they sipped their tea. Mrs. Mont asked a good many questions which Mrs. Williams had no difficulty in answering. The mental picture which Mrs. Mont formed of the *kibbutz* was somewhat at variance with the reality. She gathered that the young gentlemen occupied the top floor, the young ladies the floor below. Like East and West it seemed that never—or hardly ever—the twain met, except at meal times.

Furthermore, all the young gentlemen were inclined to be studious and rather shy—not nearly as lively, Mrs. Williams hinted, as the young men of her generation used to be. It just showed you, she pointed out, what a lot of piffle was put about by the papers and the telly about the permissiveness—Mrs. Williams called it the permission-ness—of the present day society.

But Mrs. Williams, like the artist she was, was careful not to overcook her theme—she went on to describe the three other young ladies and how pretty they looked in these modern fashions and how now and again—but surprisingly seldom, really—all eight of the *kibbutz* tenants might go out together to the pictures or a concert or something like that. But generally speaking the curtain between East and West remained down.

" One of the young men is known as ' Tubby ', isn't he?" Mrs. Mont remarked. " What is he like?"

" Oh that'll be Mr. Weatherstone—he's the shyest of the lot," Mrs. Williams said. (So Miss Denise had told her mother something about Mr. Tubby, she thought —she'd have to be careful and say the same things about him then.) " He's fat and jolly—just like a big schoolboy, really. I'll tell you something, ma'am, though maybe I shouldn't—I sometimes think he's got a notion of Miss Denise. Only he's that shy he'll never let on." She shook her head sympathetically. " No, he'll never get anywhere with girls, Mr. Weatherstone won't, 'cos of his shyness. Painful it is. You'd be sorry for him at times, ma'am. But don't tell Miss Denise what I said—"

"No of course not," Mrs. Mont said, smiling. The picture that Mrs. Williams had drawn was one that pleased her—Denise attracting young men but also causing them self-consciousness and a certain amount of awe. The child was only twenty, there was plenty of time for a more sophisticated affair when a really suitable young man came along. In the meantime Tubby sounded just right to practise on. Mrs. Mont saw her daughter as an angler practising with tiddlers in order not to miss the big one.

"Your tea was delicious," Mrs. Mont said. "And now—a quick look at Denise's room and then I really must be off if I want to miss the evening traffic rush."

"Of course, ma'am," Mrs. Williams said.

She took her visitor upstairs. Mrs. Mont did indeed prove to be a drawer-opener and a looker-under-pillows, She lifted each pillow in turn with a fine casualness, indeed almost in a fit of absentmindedness, but her eye carefully noted Denise's nightie and Olga's very feminine pyjamas. She glanced into the shower cubicle and the wardrobe. She pulled out every drawer in the place.

And then, just as she was about to go, from one of the small top drawers of the dressing-table she drew something out and gave a sudden exclamation.

"Good heavens—cigars," she cried. "*Cigars!*" Again she said it exactly as Lady Bracknell said "A *handbag?*"

Mrs. Williams (who momentarily feared Mrs. Mont had discovered the pill or something equally disastrous) said calmly, "Ah yes, ma'am—it's Miss Beloff's one little vice, as you might say. She does like the odd cigar of an evening. They say it's quite common among ladies nowadays—and not just young ladies either."

" So I believe," Mrs. Mont said with relief. (She had, as a matter of fact, often had the urge to try one of her husband's cigars herself, just once, but so far had resisted the temptation.) " I wouldn't call it a vice—more a foible, don't you think?"

" I can't say as I hold with it myself," Mrs. Williams said a little stiffly.

" It's all a matter of taste, I suppose. We musn't be too inflexible, must we? And now I really must be going, Mrs.—?"

" Williams, ma'am."

" Well, Mrs. Williams, you've been most kind. Please tell Denise I called."

" I'll do that—though I don't see her every day," Mrs. Williams said. " It's been a pleasure, I'm sure."

As they were taking leave of each other in the hall Tubby made an untimely entrance in the doorway, returning rather earlier than usual from his launderettes. He grinned at Mrs. Williams and went past them towards the stairs. Mrs. Mont raised an enquiring eyebrow at Mrs. Williams. The eyebrow plainly asked, ' Is this the young man Tubby?' (Oh Gawd, Mrs. Williams thought, couldn't the young bugger have waited a couple of minutes longer——now I'll have to introduce them.)

" Oh, Mr. Weatherstone," Mrs. Williams called, stopping Tubby in his tracks, " this is Mrs. Mont, Miss Denise's mother."

Tubby turned back. His pink face took on a momentary look of uncertainty—it could have been shyness but was actually the normal reaction of any young fellow meeting for the first time one of the parents of the girl with whom he is currently sleeping. But Mrs. Williams's eyelid quivered at him and that reassured him.

" We've been talking about you," Mrs. Williams explained archly. " I've been telling her how shy you are with girls."

"How do you do, Mrs. Mont?" Tubby said, shaking hands. (No one could have accused Tubby of being slow in the uptake.) " I—er—Miss Denise has mentioned you —not that I—er—see much of her—"

" Maybe she'll bring you down sometime—we live at Strawberry Hill, you know," Mrs. Mont said.

" I'd like that very much. It's—er—awfully nice to meet you."

" Nice to meet you, young man," Mrs. Mont said. " And now I simply *must* be off."

They watched her go down the steps. When she was out of earshot Mrs. Williams said, " You did that a treat, Mr. Tubby. You should be on stage, you should really. And now you can come up and help me carry your things back."

As Mrs. Mont, reassured by her visit, walked towards the bus stop, she reflected, he's quite a personable young man—but he'll never get himself a girl until he learns to conquer his shyness. About Mrs. Williams she felt rather more concern. The woman had all the symptoms of a heart condition. No one could get so breathless just making a cup of tea unless they had cardiac trouble. Such an admirable type, too—obviously one of the old school. . . .

It was Tuesday evening—time for another visit to The Blue Hound.

Nothing had changed. Piggy climbed the back stairs and there was Fred sitting at the table waiting for her, a half empty glass of whisky at his elbow. From the kitchen came the smell of bacon and eggs frying.

Yet something had changed—her father. He looked about twenty years older than on her last visit a week ago. His mouth was looser and the lower lids of his eyes seemed to have fallen away from the eyeballs so that they looked like some obscene intestine turned inside out. One end of his handlebars moustache was caught between his lips as if he had been sucking it.

Piggy went over and kissed him on the forehead. He roused himself and she realised he had been in a semistupor.

"Hullo, Fred," she said, "are you all right?"

"Fine—top of the bill," he said and cackled. "They wouldn't dare put us lower down—Fearless Flying Fred and Big-Boobs Vicky, the peerless pair. Have a snifter, Peg."

He poured some whisky into a teacup and pushed it towards her. She didn't want it but she said, "Thanks, Fred," and pretended to sip it.

"That's my girl," he said, his voice slurring. "Getting to like your tipple, eh? Never believe them when they tell you it's bad for you. Have a good belly-laugh when they say, 'stop drinking, or else—'." He stared at her from under his eyebrows but apparently had difficulty in focusing. Even his wagging finger seemed out of control. "Stop drinking—Christ, that's a laugh. What else is there?—nothing—sweet damn all—"

Suddenly he dozed off, his brief coherence over. Piggy sat and watched him. His head gave little spasmodic jerks. He reminded her of a dog they had once had, whose legs twitched in sleep; she had always imagined it was chasing dream rabbits. Once or twice now Fred smiled. She wondered what he was thinking about. Maybe he's shooting down Messerschmitts, she thought. She wouldn't have disturbed him for anything in the world. If he really was up there in imagination, throwing his plane about the sky, that meant he was young and healthy and happy again, doing the one thing in all his life he had done well.

Vicky came in with her tray of bacon and eggs. "Hullo, Peg," she said. She put the teapot and the three plates down and glanced at Fred. "God, is he away again?" she said. "I don't know why I bother cooking food for him. Half the time he can't touch it. I suppose the lining of his stomach's completely gone."

Piggy said quietly, "Maybe we should just let him doze. I don't think he's too well—"

"Well?" Vicky repeated and laughed brassily. "How the hell could he be well? Never a day passes now that he doesn't get into his second bottle. You're lucky— you don't have to live with him. He's just a sodden pig."

"He'll hear you," Piggy said.

"No—not when he goes off like that. He won't wake up until someone prods him—and then it'll only be for a couple of seconds. He'll just sit hunched up there until I help him off to bed. God knows why I don't leave him to freeze to death. He would, you know—there's no heat left in his body. One of these nights I will, so help me."

"He was a good man once—good and brave," Piggy said.

"He killed a lot of men. If that's good, then I suppose Fred Farthingale was good."

Piggy and her mother chatted desultorily through the meal, though they had nothing to say to each other,

69

nothing in common. It was completely mechanical. You opened your mouth and something came out. Still, Piggy could not help feeling a certain sympathy for Vicky. Anyone living with Fred certainly deserved sympathy. She wondered if things would have turned out differently if he had married someone else. Or was he predestined to destroy himself?

She cut her visit a little shorter than usual. There was no point in sitting there manufacturing conversation with Vicky. Fred's plate of bacon and eggs still lay before him untouched.

As Piggy rose to go Vicky said, " Prod your father and he'll become conscious long enough to say good-bye."

Piggy went over and prodded Fred gently on the shoulder. He only grunted so she prodded him again a little harder. This time he wakened and stared at her.

" Christ, if it isn't Peg," he said.

" I'll come back and see you next week," Piggy said.

" Jesus Christ—a week?" he seemed dazed. " A lot can happen in a week. A week's a helluva long time, Peg."

She kissed him on the forehead. He whispered something. It sounded like, " I'm frightened, Peg—I'm frightened." But it couldn't have been that. Fred Farthingale would never say that. She asked quickly, " What was that?" But he had dropped off to sleep again and she hadn't the heart to try to wake him.

Vicky came with her to the door.

" I'd better tell you," Vicky said. " I didn't mean to, but now I'd better. Your father wakens up every night about two and vomits his guts up. Sometimes he chokes so that you'd swear he was on the way out. I got the doctor and he says Fred'll go in one of these coughing bouts. He'll just choke to death—choke on his own vomit —and there's no way of stopping him."

Piggy didn't even feel like crying. There was something so inevitable about Fred's self-destruction that sorrow would have been pointless.

She said, " If I can help in any way—"

" No one can help your father," Vicky said. " It might happen tonight or not for six months, that's what the doctor said. If I had my choice, it would be tonight— and I'm not being unkind when I say that. Look after yourself—I don't know why you bother to come, Peg, honest to God I don't."

Max Rickaby was driving his ancient MG along the farther reaches of Caledonian Road. He was in quest of orders for stationery requisites and the back seat was stuffed with samples. It was a fine sunny day—the sort of day that always convinced Max, for the moment, that his job was a cushy one.

Max reckoned to do about a dozen to fifteen calls a day and to complete the full circuit once every couple of months. Most of his customers were steady. It wasn't so much a matter of hard selling as just dropping in to book orders. He usually got about ten sizable orders a day and this gave him a very fair commission to supplement his small basic salary. Actually supplement is the wrong word for the commission was four or five times as much as his salary. Firms were cunning about how they worked. They didn't mind paying out commission on sales but they took good care not to be burdened with big overheads when sales struck a bad week. That was why basic salaries were so small. It was really the traveller who took the brunt of a bad week rather than the firm. Still, Max was popular with the buyers and the goods were quality stuff so he didn't strike many bad weeks.

At the moment, however, Max's mind wasn't on business at all—or at least not on that sort of business. He was calculating when the next change-round of sleeping partners was due. It came round every three months and he reckoned next week would be the week.

He ran through in his mind the present set-up—Piggy and Willie Torr, Olga and Ted Allard, Denise and Tubby, Sue and himself. That meant that in the normal rota progression he would move forward to Piggy (it was always the girls who stayed put and the men who changed rooms).

Now, Max liked Piggy, he liked her very much. She might not be a raging beauty like the other three but he found her face attractive. In bed she had no deficiencies. Sue, his present partner, was also splendid there —athletic but splendid. In fact all four girls were absolute tops in bed each in her own slightly different way. No reasonable man could possibly pick a fault in any of them. Yet Max found himself on this sunny morning, when his head should have been full of business thoughts, wondering how he could wangle the room-sharing rota so that it would bring him round again to Olga out of his turn.

He had no idea how Olga herself would feel about it. He wondered if the girls had any strong preference. If they had, they didn't talk about it to him, not even in moments of greatest intimacy. He had tried to pump Sue that night of the party but she had answered only in generalities.

He felt—as a matter of realism, not conceit—that he

72

was the best-looking of the four men. Tubby was—well, too tubby. Willie had his bent nose. Ted probably came second (though, personally, Max didn't fancy beards much, perhaps because he had made the experiment with disappointing results). Bowling along the Caledonian Road Max checked up on his looks by making faces at himself in the driving mirror. By turns he made his expression stern, melting, appealing, bold, masterful, humorous. He even threw in a monster-from-outer-space expression. Then he noticed that a policeman on points duty was looking at him oddly so he blinked as if it was due to the sun getting in his eyes.

He cudgelled his brains to discover what Olga had got that the others hadn't but couldn't pick out any one quality. All the girls had essentially *nice* natures. He fell back on the old trick explanation—they were all equal but Olga was somehow more equal than the others. While he was stopped at a traffic light the idea occurred to him that it might be due to her Russian blood.

Presently he turned into the car park of a big retail firm which was his first call. He switched off the engine and sat for a moment wondering if there really could be anything in the Russian blood theory. Then he gathered up his order book and brief case containing a few selected samples and went up to the office.

Even while he was talking to the firm's buyer his mind was only half on business. Instead of writing in the order book 3 *doz. reams best quality monogrammed notepaper* he wrote 3 *doz. Olga Beloffs* and had to tear out the page hastily and begin again.

All that day as he made his rounds he kept turning over schemes to fiddle the rota so that it would give him more than his fair share of Olga. It wouldn't be easy.

c*   73

He had a notion that if a Gallop poll were taken of the four men's favourite sleeping partner, Olga would win four-nil. There would be no don't-knows. So his reasons would have to be convincing. He couldn't get away with just saying, 'We started a series of poetry readings in bed last time and now we want to finish it' or anything like that.

Then it occurred to him that under the present three-month rota you always got the same girl in the same season—spring would always bring you the same girl as the previous spring and so on. There might be an opportunity for a fiddle here. It might sound perfectly reasonable to suggest that if you had a certain girl, say, this summer, you'd like to try her out at a different season next time. So why not make it a four-month cycle? That would necessitate starting all over again. And maybe, since it would be he who'd brought the point up, they might let him arrange the new rota. If so, he'd make sure to start off with Olga himself.

By the time he parked his car in the mews that evening, Max's conscience had got the upper hand. The wangle simply wasn't on. It would be disloyal to the tenets of the *kibbutz*. Worse still, even if the others let him get away with it someone was sure to catch on that he was doing a fiddle and that would cause simmering offence (Max really did hate to hurt anyone).

So he finally decided, 'Christ no, I'll just have to make do with my fair ration of Olga. After all, they're all smashing partners—nine hundred and ninety-nine men out of a thousand would be green with envy of me—and the thousandth would be a queer.'

He had had an unworthy impulse, an attack of human frailty. But now he had put it behind him. He had a strong sense of what was moral and ethically right, had Max.

In accordance with the rules of the *kibbutz* the rota switched the following week. The new order was Piggy and Max, Olga and Willie, Denise and Ted, Sue and Tubby. As always, nobody made any criticism.

At breakfast the next morning the phone in the hall rang. Tubby, already finished, went to answer it. He came back to the door and said, " For you, Piggy."

She was gone for about five minutes. When she came back she stared at her cornflakes unseeingly. Presently they saw that she was crying.

Sue, her fellow-worker in the boutique, got up quietly and went to her and put an arm round her.

" Piggy—what's wrong?"

Piggy looked up at her with faraway, tear-filled eyes.

" My father died during the night."

There were murmurs of dismay and sympathy and then everyone sat in silence, not looking at Piggy.

Presently Max, her room-sharer, asked quietly, " Is there anything I can do to help? I can easily take the day off and make any arrangements that need making—"

Piggy shook her head.

" Thanks, Max—but mother will look after everything."

Sue said, " Don't worry about the boutique or anything. I'll explain to Uncle Ikey why you're taking a few days off. We'll manage fine."

Everyone was uncomfortable, wanting to do or say something helpful (it is not easy for young people to rub shoulders with death). Someone murmured, " He must have been a wonderful person—"

Piggy looked up fiercely.

"He was—oh he was!" she cried. "He was a hero of the Battle of Britain—he shot down more enemy planes than anyone else in his squadron—twenty-two Messerschmitts—"

They were silent again, feeling clumsy and trying to picture this old-time pilot throwing his primitive plane about the sky, bravely fighting against an equally brave foe in a war that had finished long before anyone in that room was born.

Willie said, "Would—would you like us four men to go to the funeral, Piggy? Just say if you'd like that—"

Piggy shook her head.

"No, Willie, no—it'll be private."

"You'd better lie down for half an hour," Ted said.

"I'll take you up," one of the girls offered. Everyone was still feeling clumsy.

"No—I must go to mother—"

None of them knew exactly where her home was. Max said, "I'll drive you there—"

But again Piggy shook her head. "Thanks, Max, but I'd rather go alone."

Sue got her up on her feet then and they moved towards the door. The others were silent, watching helplessly. Suddenly Piggy felt an enormous sense of something dishonest and phoney—something that Fred, the old real Fred, simply wouldn't have countenanced.

She turned at the door and told them fiercely, "He *was* a hero once—but not when he died. He married a barmaid and became an alcoholic and their life together was sordid and horrible. He died in his sleep from an overdose of drink. I'm glad he's gone, glad for his sake —glad, glad, glad— !"

76

She turned and went out alone. She felt better now. A public pretence would do her father no honour. Her private memories were not to be shared, not even in the *kibbutz*. As she went up the stairs she could almost hear Fred cackle his approbation.

The three girls came up to see her but Piggy told them she'd rather be alone. She lay on the bed for half an hour and cried quietly. Then she got up and washed her face and went by underground to The Blue Hound. She stayed with Vicky until the funeral was over. They spoke quietly, reasonably to each other and between them they saw that Fred made a decent exit.

Once Vicky said, " He left me the pub. His money he left to you—about fifteen hundred, I think. Is that all right?"

Piggy nodded without interest.

" Yes—yes, of course."

There were three wreaths. One was from Vicky and Piggy, the second had a card on it which said, ' With Love and Sympathy from the *Kibbutz*.' The third simply said ' From Uncle Ikey.' Reading it, Piggy cried again, briefly, for the first time since that morning when she had got the phone call.

Next day she returned to the *kibbutz* and life went on just as usual. Except that Piggy's visits to The Blue Hound became less and less frequent until after a while they ceased altogether.

FOUR

THE PROPRIETORS of the launderettes were giving a dance. Not to the employees in general but to the higher-ups of the launderette world, their business associates, wives and girl-friends. It was to be a ballroom, dinner-jacket affair. Tubby, as manager of the chain, just scraped into the invitation list—the card said ' Mr. Weatherstone and partner '.

Tubby, like most fat men, was a good ballroom dancer. He and Olga were the only members of the *kibbutz* who could do ballroom dancing. Olga, perhaps because of her spell of ballet training, could fit in with any sort of partner, even the type who threw his girl about like a yo-yo, slinging her between his legs and over his shoulder. But it was unlikely there would be any of that sort at the launderette dance.

Tubby didn't often take any of the *kibbutz* girls out in the evening. but he wanted to make a good impression as a dancer on this occasion so he decided to ask Olga. They had danced together somewhere before and knew each other's form. So when Tubby asked her if she'd care to go, Olga said, " Oh golly, wouldn't I just, Tubby."

When they came down that evening dressed for the occasion they eyed each other approvingly. Tubby looked impressive, if a trifle aldermanic, in his tuxedo, which seldom got an airing. Olga had on a long close-fitting flame-coloured dress, low cut in front and back and with a belt of big linked gilt bangles. Her fair hair cascaded like cloth of gold against the flame.

Tubby whistled and said, " Smashing—pity it hides your legs, though."

" Don't pretend you've forgotten what they look like," Olga said. " You've been over them often enough one way and another to have a blue print in your head."

" True," Tubby acknowledged, " true."

They took a taxi to the hall, which was the premises of a West End club taken over for the night. There was a buffet and a well-stocked bar with all drinks on the house. It was quite a small gathering composed for the most part of prosperous-looking middle-aged and elderly bald-headed men whose wives, oddly enough, all seemed to be in their twenties. Tubby introduced Olga to everybody he knew but he also took good care to keep her to himself.

For the next three hours Tubby and Olga danced almost continuously, except for a few visits to the buffet and many to the bar. The floor and the band were excellent. Tubby on a dance floor lost all his brashness and became an elegant and accomplished artist. Olga herself was the sort of performer who could make even a bad partner look polished. When her partner really *was* polished, as now, they became the sort of combination that quite often causes run-of-the-mill dancers to say to their partners, ' Let's sit this one out and just watch

79

those two.' That sort of attention, Tubby felt, did his business prospects no harm.

For both of them it was a splendid three hours. They didn't talk much or compliment each other while they were dancing. Both knew, without any trace of self-conceit, that they happened to be 'naturals' in this particular line of country, so each just concentrated on enjoying to the maximum their mutual expertise.

By midnight their synchronisation had attained a standard usually only to be seen at championships. This was all the more pleasing to Tubby because it scared off predatory males. Only two summoned up the courage to ask Olga for a dance. Neither was particularly good but she made them look better than they had ever looked before. Even so, they realised they were moving in a stratum for which they were not really fitted and neither aspired to such heights a second time.

By one o'clock, admittedly, a slight deterioration—perceptible only to themselves—had set in in the Tubby-Olga combination and Olga had had to take over some of the male duty of steering. This was simply due to Tubby becoming a little tight and in no way diminished the pleasure of what had gone before.

Olga was the slightest bit tiddly herself, her intake having been perhaps a quarter of Tubby's. She couldn't help noticing that when they did a sharp turn now the lights had a momentary tendency to run together. Fortunately it didn't matter because everyone else seemed to be a lot drunker and most of them were sprawling at the tables round the floor. However, after one last exhibition foxtrot—which the band themselves clapped as well as the other spectators—Olga thought it prudent to steer Tubby towards a vacant table. On the way he collected another Scotch-and-soda. He offered to get one for Olga but she declined. She felt the amount she had had was just about right.

When they sat down Tubby drank his whisky straight off as if it had been a tomato juice. His eyes were beginning to have the look of a man who has just discovered he needs spectacles.

" God," he said, " you're good—s'matter of fact you're abso-bloody-lutely marvellous."

" You're not so bad yourself," Olga said.

" Tell you a secret—I'm in awe of you." He was chewing his words a bit now.

Olga giggled.

" You were never in awe of a girl in your life, Tubby Weatherstone—"

" No—no—honest—I'm in awe of you," Tubby insisted. " Gigantic, paralysing awe. Always have been—always. Didn't know that, did you—?"

" If you're paralysed it's not with awe," Olga said. " Maybe you took that last drink too fast."

" *In vino veritas*," Tubby mumbled. He seemed gratified at having thought of the tag because he repeated it again. " *In vino veritas*. It's true—true. Tubby's in awe of Olga."

" You're fibbing," Olga said giggling again.

" *If* you please." Tubby spoke with great dignity but the dignity was somewhat spoiled by an immense burp. " Oh—pardon."

" Are you all right—?"

" Course I'm all right—think I'm tight or something—?"

" You're joking—aren't you, Tubby?"

" Joking? What about—?"

" About being in awe of me."

" No, it's God's truth. If only you'd listen—"

" But I am listening—"

" All right—okay—you're listening. Know why I'm in awe of you—?"

" No."

" 'Cos we're at opposite bloody ends of the *kibbutz* scale. I see it clearer now than ever before—*in vino veritas*. All the others are—hic—good average *kibbutzers*. Me—I'm way below average—not up to it. I'm really a fat selfish bugger. But you—you're way above average. You and me—we're not really *kibbutzers* at all. You're too nice—I'm not nice enough—"

" Here, just hold on," Olga said. " Really, Tubby—you're a wonderful dancer but now you're talking drivel—"

" Not talking drivel."

" You are, Tubby, you are."

" So you don't believe I'm a fat selfish bugger—?"

Olga patted his hand.

" You may be a little fat but you're definitely not a selfish bugger—"

Tubby thumped the table.

" But I am, I tell you—I am—I am—"

" Honestly, Tubby, you're not."

Tubby gave a hopeless shrug.

" See what I mean? You're so good you can't see the bad in others."

Olga blew out her cheeks and gave an exasperated puff.

" Oh for heaven's sake, Tubby. Now I'll tell *you* something. Sometimes I have to make a terrific effort myself just to keep up to the standard of the other girls, let alone get ahead of them. Just think of them—Denise and Sue and Piggy—they're marvellous—"

"Ha! Who's talking drivel now?—drivel, absolute bloody drivel," Tubby said. He even seemed on the point of becoming tearful. "Don't get me wrong—I'm not saying the other girls aren't marvellous—they are. But I'm saying you're super-marvellous. That's not all—now we come to the odd bit. Have you noticed if there's a discussion or anything, I wait to hear which side you're on and then I take the opposite. Have you noticed that, eh?—Have you noticed—?"

"No, I have not—"

"Well, you just want to start noticing. Because that's exactly what I do. And you know why? 'Cos it's a—hic—defence mechanism. It's the only way I can assert myself. It makes me feel I'm someone, contradicting you —not much, but someone. You get it? And I'll have to keep on doing it too. That's—hic—that's a hell of a thing, isn't it? I know you're right all the time but I'll still bloody well have to contradict you. Like Judas Iscariot. That's the sort of stupid disgusting bugger I am. You do understand what I'm talking about, don't you—?"

"No I don't," Olga said. The lights were still running together a bit.

"Oh Christ," Tubby groaned.

"I think you're tiddly, Tubby," Olga said.

She liked the sound of the last two words but they were a little tricky to say so she practised them to herself two or three times in an undertone, "Tiddly Tubby, tiddly Tubby."

"Can't hear what you're saying," Tubby complained. "Oh God, maybe I'm going deaf—"

"You're tiddly, Tubby—"

"I am not—the Weatherstones never get tiddly. You find a Weatherstone—you got yourself a man can hold his liquor." He stared at her broodingly and a slightly cunning look came into his eyes. "Tell me, when we were room-sharing was I any good—?"

"Yes, Tubby, you were very good—"

"Did you really enjoy it—?"

"Yes, Tubby, really."

"Sometimes I felt you were just pretending to enjoy it to please me."

The lights were beginning to get steadier again now. Olga said gently, "If I didn't really enjoy making love I just wouldn't make it."

"Honest to God—?"

"Honest to God, Tubby."

"I'm a worm," Tubby said.

Olga took his hand in both of hers.

"You can't go out with a worm and have a lovely time dancing with him. That proves you're not a worm."

"Oh Christ," Tubby said again.

She patted his hand. She hoped he wouldn't talk any more now because he was saying things he would regret tomorrow. The lights were absolutely steady now.

She said, "Time to go home, Tubby. All good things must come to an end. Hadn't I better say good-bye to our host? Do you know which one he is?"

Tubby screwed up his eyes and looked round the hall, obviously making a really terrific effort to focus.

"That man there," he said, pointing. "That bald-headed cove. That's our host—that's the one."

"What's his name—?"

84

" Oh Christ, I can't remember."

Olga rose and went over to the man. She was delighted to find she could walk perfectly straight. Actually there were two men sitting at a table. They were talking together and one of them, a stout bald little man, was saying with a lisp. " Yes, he's a lovely boy—I had him last Thursday in Hyde Park." Then he noticed Olga and looked at her enquiringly.

Olga said, " I'm not sure which of you is our host, but we're going now and I just wanted to say thank you very much, we had a lovely time."

The stout bald little man waved a beringed hand at her and said, " Delighted you could come—you sure can dance, lady." Then he went on talking to his companion as if she wasn't there so Olga went back to Tubby.

Once she had got him on his feet he was quite manageable. In the taxi he dozed off, his head on her breast. He looked rather like an overgrown baby so she put her arm round him and talked to him as she would have talked to a baby. She wasn't sure whether he heard her or not but he made a small snuffling noise such as a contented baby makes.

When they reached the *kibbutz* the taxi-driver helped her winkle him out and once his feet touched the pavement he sobered up manfully and paid the fare in quite a grand manner.

They went up the steps of 32 with their arms about each other. Sue and Willie, their respective room-sharers, had thoughtfully waited up in case they might need a helping hand. They were playing chess together in the sitting-room. Just as Tubby and Olga were the only good ballroom-dancers in the *kibbutz*, so Willie and Sue were the only good chess players—indeed, the only ones who could play at all. Willie had the white pieces and Olga noticed that there were six white pieces left but only four black.

"Had a good dance?" Sue asked. She was sitting with her arms folded studying the board and was so absorbed she didn't look up.

"Lovely," Olga said. "Tubby's really terrific on the floor." She was still holding him upright.

Willie looked up and grinned at Olga.

"He smells terrific too," he said, but he said it in a friendly way. "Want any help?"

"No," Olga said, "Tubby's fine. Aren't you, Tubby?"

"I'm a worm," Tubby said.

"What was that again?" Sue asked, looking up now from the chessboard.

"He's only joking," Olga said.

Suddenly Tubby began to grin foolishly all over his face. He was sagging at the knees and pretending to be on the point of collapse.

"Who's going to put me to bed?" he asked

Willie said resignedly, "Okay, Tubby—sit down a jiffy till I finish Sue off. Then I'll see you all right."

"Don't want you," Tubby said. "Want one of the girls."

Sue looked up again and smiled at Olga.

"Would you mind, Olga?" she asked. "If I go now I'll have to concede to Willie."

"That's all right," Olga said. "Come on, Tubby."

She took Tubby up to Sue's room and helped him undress. While he was struggling into his pyjamas she folded his discarded clothes and put them away in the way she remembered he liked. Then she turned down the bedclothes. While she was doing that Tubby suddenly came to violent life again. He grabbed her and did a prancing polka with her round the room. She felt sure they must waken the rest of the *kibbutz* if not the whole neighbourhood. They circled the room three or four times and then Olga said, " Dancing's over, Tubby —the band's packing up."

She manoeuvred him towards the bed and gave him a gentle push. He collapsed into it and she covered him up. But his hand came out again and patted the bed.

" Getting in beside me—?"

" Not tonight, Josephine," Olga said, " that's Sue's place."

" Gimme a kiss, then." She kissed him and he asked, " Did I talk a lot of nonsense tonight—?"

" We both did," Olga said. " I don't remember what we said but it was great fun and I had a lovely time." She kissed him again. " Thanks for everything, Tubby. You're a terrific dancer, absolutely tops. Now go to sleep like a good boy."

" Nice Olga," Tubby murmured.

He seemed to drop straight off. She went downstairs again, a little tiredly now. Willie was putting away the chessmen and Sue was just bringing in three cups of coffee on a tray.

" He did me again but one day I'll lick him, just wait and see if I don't," Sue said. " Took my queen when she wasn't looking. Barefaced rape—you can trust no one. Well, how's his lordship?"

" Asleep, I think."

" It looks like a restful night for yours truly," Sue remarked.

Olga and Willie laughed and Willie said, "We thought the ceiling was coming down. I wanted to dash up but Sue thought it was just a goodnight waltz."

"A polka, actually," Olga said.

They talked a little longer while they drank their coffee then they said good-night and went upstairs.

In the bedroom Willie didn't ask Olga anything about her night with Tubby. He just took her in his arms and kissed her gently and asked, "Glad to be back with Uncle Willie?"

She said, "Tubby really is a super dancer—he got a little tight but he was sweet." She wondered why she hadn't given him the satisfaction of a direct answer. Because she realised she really was glad to be back with Willie.

In the staff-room behind the boutique Sue was finishing the snack lunch which Rebecca had prepared for her. Before her on the table lay a letter. She was alone in the staff-room and she kept reading the letter as she ate—reading it for perhaps the twentieth time since it had arrived that morning.

The letter was from a village in the north of England and it said :

Dear Susan,

Both your father and I have made up our minds. We have asked God's help about it and He has answered us. It is not just like the Prodigal Son, because a daughter is different from a son and that makes it a lot more serious. If you come home within three days of getting this letter we will still take you back. But if you fail to appear you had better make up your mind never to come home again at all, for as God-fearing people humbly trying to follow Christ we have a reputation to uphold among our fellow Christians. This is not a decision we have come to lightly or on our own. It has come directly to us from the Almighty, but only because your father and I have spent long hours on our knees seeking His guidance. Our knees are sore from kneeling but it is nothing compared with Christ's agony on the cross.

We still cannot understand, Susan, what possessed you to leave a Christian home and go to a place like London, which is full of sin and temptation and where we cannot watch over you. Least of all can we understand you working for a Jew. Can you not realise that these are the people who crucified Christ? Or do you simply not care?

Then there is your attitude towards ourselves. It it not as if we had ever been unkind or unreasonable. Unfortunately you could never appreciate that the discipline we imposed on you was for your own good and that the only true happiness lies in submission to Christ's yolk.

However, we are still prepared to forgive your ingratitude provided you return home within three days. I may say we have spoken to the minister and he agrees with us that it would not be seemly to let condonation of your conduct run on indefinitely. He feels we may even already have erred too far on the side of leniency.

So it is three days, Susan—or cut yourself off for ever from your Christian home. I would beseech you at this late hour to remember what the Psalmist said : "Stand in awe and sin not; commune with your

own heart upon your bed, and be still " (Psalms 4 :4).
The word bed is, we feel, of great significance here.

Whichever way you decide, we shall of course always continue to pray for you. It is a wonderful feeling to know that we are in the right and that Christ's hand is on ours, guiding the pen as we write.

Yours in the Master,

Mother.

P.S. Even if we knew for certain that you are living in sin (as we very much fear) we would still intercede in prayer for you because even though you may be beyond worldly help, your Heavenly Father has the power to redeem sinners even up to the very mouth of Hell itself. Amen.

Sue sat for a while staring at the letter. She tried very hard, as she had done countless times in the past, to feel sympathy for her parents' point of view but found that she still could not. So she rose and got her notepaper and a ballpoint from a drawer and wrote her reply :

Dear Mummy,

Thank you for your letter. I am sorry I do not feel it would be right for me to return home. We would only keep quarrelling and wear each other out.

I am among friendly people here and do not feel that I am living in sin. You will think it odd but I am happier than I ever was before. I do not think there is any point in writing anything more.

Much love to you and Daddy

Sue.

She addressed an envelope and put the letter inside and sealed and stamped it. There would just be time to post it before she was due to relieve Piggy in the boutique.

As she went through the shop she called to Piggy, telling her she was going to the pillar-box at the corner and would be back in a minute. Piggy waved back to her and called, " No hurry."

At the door Sue paused momentarily at a mirror to examine herself in profile. She was wearing a new bra that was supposed to make the bust look smaller but she couldn't see much difference.

Denise Mont and Ted Allard were walking along Oxford Street and heads were turning to look at the redhead and her bearded companion.

Denise wore a big sombrero, a black kerchief round her neck with polka dots on it the colour of her hair, a green lumber-shirt and Mexican gaucho trousers with chaps and leather belt (all purchased not from the Oxford Street store where she worked but from Uncle Ikey's boutique). Her green leather boots had little silver spurs on them and although you might have doubted her ability to throw a steer you couldn't have denied she was quite an eyeful. The whole ensemble was finished off with big dark glasses.

Ted, in polo-neck sweater and jeans of more sober hue, looked a fit escort for her, which is saying a lot. Ted wore casual clothes when he was looking after the lighting for a rehearsal; if, in addition, he was down to attend conferences or anything like that where one of the B.B.C. higher-ups might sit in, he usually wore a suit and tie.

Denise chuckled suddenly.

"I forgot to tell you about what happened the week before last—oh Ted, it was a giggle. Mummy called at the *kibbutz* when only Mrs. Williams was there. Mummy said she happened to be passing and had dropped in on the spur of the moment—Mummy's a wonderful liar but Mrs. Williams is no mug. She parked Mummy in the sitting-room, tore upstairs like a mad thing and cleared all Tubby's stuff from my room into Olga's—it was Tubby and me then. Then she collected Olga's and dumped them in mine—"

"I know," Ted said, grinning. "She slipped up on at least one detail in her hurry. Olga found a pair of panties that weren't hers—"

"Oh yes—you were with Olga then, weren't you? What did she say—?"

"She just held them up and exclaimed, 'Good lord, where did these come from?—they aren't mine.' I took a look and said, 'Try Denise.' Tell me, would it have mattered all that much if your mother had found out about the set-up at the *kibbutz*?"

Denise considered for a moment.

"Not really. She'd have raged for a week, grumbled for another week, and then said resignedly, 'Oh well, if the girl wants to live like something in a farmyard, it's her life'."

"She sounds sensible."

"She's sweet. As old-fashioned as be damned, of course—but sweet."

They sauntered on in the early summer sunlight and Denise suddenly chuckled again.

"Can't you just hear Mrs. Williams's 'Oh Gawd!'?"

"Yes—in that fruity, randy voice of hers."

"She's all for the *kibbutz* system, bless her. I didn't see her till yesterday and when she told me about Mummy's visit I gave her ten bob. She didn't want to take it. She kept asking, 'You're sure it won't leave you short, dearie—?'"

"That's a cue for me to stand you lunch, if ever I heard one—"

"It wasn't—but if you insist—"

"All right, I'll let myself be imposed on," Ted said. "To celebrate us being together again."

"You like it this way—?"

Ted grinned. "To be honest, I like it any way."

"Farmyard rooster," Denise said in a friendly voice.

They had met quite by accident. Ted had happened to be passing as Denise came out of her store for the lunch break. (There was a canteen in the store but Denise didn't always use it.) Ted had come up behind her and linked up his finger with one of hers, just as he would have linked with Olga or Sue or Piggy. She had turned quickly and said, "Oh it's you, Ted," and held up her mouth to be kissed, just as any of the other three would almost certainly have done. That was the great thing about the *kibbutz*, Ted told himself. Nobody belonged to anybody. The room-sharing rota was only an arrangement of convenience and wasn't intended to restrict freedom at other hours of the twenty-four.

They went into Stella Alpina in North Audley Street and had a light Italian lunch in Alpine surroundings.

"We're doing a new series at the B.B.C." Ted said, making conversation across the table. "Just about ordinary young people trying to make a go of life. Rather like ourselves, really. Older people accuse them of living like animals. The lot in the play haven't much ex-

93

perience. Make mistakes, of course. But in the end they find a formula that suits them. The lighting's damned tricky."

"Why don't you try to get Willie in on something like that?" Denise said, munching a morsel of pasta. "It might give him ideas for a plot—"

"I did try. I spoke to one of the drama producers. He said to bring Willie along sometime and he'd have a chat with him. But Willie wouldn't go. Swears he can't get his ideas by talking to people or wandering round the British Museum or anything like that. He's tried it and it's no bloody good. The way his mind works, ideas have to come from personal experience."

"Poor Willie, he won't go far on that," Denise said. "You'd have to be an astronaut or a spy or a famous courtesan or something, wouldn't you—?"

"No—that's what everybody thinks but it's not true. This play we're doing's about ordinary people and it'll be a smash success, you'll see. When you think of it, everybody's ordinary—even film stars. Coming up behind you in Oxford Street I thought, now *that* could be a film star—"

"Was that why you hooked on to my finger—?"

"Oh no, I knew it was you—I recognised your bottom—"

"Well, really—"

"No offence. It's a smashing bottom and you wiggle it beautifully—"

"I don't—not intentionally, anyway. It's just the way girls walk—"

"Then all I can say is some are a hell of a lot better at it than others." He handed her the menu. "What are you having to follow?"

94

Denise was still wearing her dark glasses. She took them off now to read the menu. She studied it carefully.

"Stoned peaches and ice cream—oh, and perhaps a small glass of Montepulchiano." She became conscience-stricken suddenly. "No—we'll leave out the Montepulchiano, that would be rubbing it in."

Ted waved an airy hand.

"Nothing's too pricey for a girl with a bottom like yours."

She put out her tongue at him but not really in a rude way.

"Of all the *kibbutz* men you are undoubtedly the cheekiest, Ted Allard. I used to think Tubby was. But he's just cheeky-boisterous, you're cheeky-cheeky."

Ted grinned.

"Funny thing, Olga told me that too, once."

The waiter came back and took their order and when he was gone, Denise put on her glasses again and said casually, "Talking of Olga, you said you'd give me lunch just to celebrate us being together again. You were just being gallant, weren't you?—you didn't really like switching from Olga to me, did you?"

Surprised, Ted said, "Good lord, what makes you think that?"

"Curiosity—not really bitchiness," Denise said. "But each of you four men would rather share a room with Olga than with any of the rest of us, wouldn't you? I don't know if the other girls have even thought about it. It's just something I've been wondering about—"

"You're talking through the top of your very pretty head."

Denise reached across the table and beat a tickling tattoo on the back of Ted's hand.

"Humour my curiosity, please, Ted. Honestly, I'm not being bitchy. Nobody could be bitchy about Olga. Maybe I just want to improve myself. Is she better in bed?"

"No. You're all perfect there—each different but each perfect. Cross my heart."

"All right—if you don't want to answer—"

"For you," he said, "I'll invent something. Maybe it's her Russian blood."

"I sometimes think her Russian blood began as a joke and now she keeps it up just to amuse us—"

"Well, I can't think of anything else. You'll have to invent something for yourself."

"All right, I will," Denise said. "I think you all like her best because, quite simply, she never thinks of herself. Just sit and turn that over in your mind. It's pretty fantastic. The rest of us are an averagely decent bunch but we're not in that class. Come to think of it, I can't think of any one else who is. I meant what I said absolutely literally—*she never considers herself*."

"My God," Ted said in a horrified voice, "that's tantamount to calling her a Christian. You want to watch what you say, you do really, my pet—"

"Remember your John Donne—?" Denise asked unexpectedly.

"My John who—?"

"The poet."

"So you're an intellectual, too," Ted said. "Not just a pretty bottom."

Denise ignored that.

"He said, ' Any man's death diminishes me '—"

"You've got a bit of explaining to do," Ted said.

"I know," Denise said. "I'm sorry now I started it. But what really worries me is that one day one of you men will marry Olga and take her away from the *kibbutz*. The marriage of any of our couples would diminish the *kibbutz*. It would do worse than diminish —it would be the beginning of the end. Can you have our sort of *kibbutz* with less than four couples? I doubt it. That's what really worries me, Ted."

"Then you can forget it. I swear before God the idea of marrying anyone has never entered my head. If it did I'd kick it out like I'd kick out a mad dog. I know when I'm well fixed, thank you. And I've never heard Willie or Max or Tubby ever mention it either. Marriage?—it's a dirty word."

"All right—now I can really enjoy the peaches and Montepulchiano," Denise said, looking relieved. She saw a waiter approaching at that moment and her bright face became positively radiant. Like a small girl she bounced in her seat and clapped her hands. "Here they come—oh gosh, they look gorgeous!"

It really was pleasant, Ted reflected, to be sitting there with Denise. It was this sort of thing that caused older people—women as well as men—to turn and look at her and smile delightedly at each other. When you went anywhere with Denise you always imagined—quite wrongly, of course—that maybe you yourself were attracting some of the admiring attention. In this head-turning business only Olga of the other three girls could run Denise close. But Olga did it in a slightly different way. There was always an exotic hint of the ballerina about Olga. People didn't turn to each other and talk delightedly about her. They just sat and looked at her and you could almost hear them thinking, 'What a wonderful girl—I wish I knew her.' There was, in Ted's opinion, another difference too—something that bore out what Denise had been saying. He didn't think Olga even knew anyone was looking at her. Denise wasn't stuck-up about it or anything like that but she was certainly conscious of the stir she was creating around her.

They got back to their usual chatter then and soon Ted had forgotten all about marriage which wasn't one of his favourite subjects anyway. As they parted afterwards in the street to go their separate ways Denise held up her face to him in that captivating way she had. It was both like a very small girl pouting her lips to be kissed by a favourite uncle and at the same time like a wanton deliberately seducing a shy admirer (not that there was anything shy about Ted Allard).

" Thanks for a scrumptious lunch, Ted."

Under the sombrero he kissed her lingeringly on the lips. A gentleman in a bowler hat who was passing nearly walked into a lamp-post watching them.

" I'll stand and watch you for a moment wiggling your way back towards Oxford Street," Ted said, grinning.

" You will not, you filthy rooster !"

But he did. And when she had gone fifty yards, just to show there was no ill feeling she turned and blew him another kiss.

Now Olga was writing to her parents. Her father had taken up a five-year appointment as lecturer in Scandinavian history at a Canadian university; he was half-Swedish but Olga's mother was English. They had lived together in London until Olga's father had got the Canadian appointment, then her mother had gone with him to Canada but Olga had stayed on in London because she was taking ballet lessons at the time and hoped eventually to join the Royal Ballet.

It happened to be a slack afternoon in the office of Sloane, Medway & Sloane. The typewriter was free so Olga used it for her letter. She didn't write very frequently to her parents but when she did it was usually at considerable length.

She wrote :

Dear Mom and Pop,

I hope you are both well and that Mom's arthritis is in one of its less troublesome moods. Your last letter reminded me of how long it is since I wrote. The Beloffs are shocking correspondents, aren't they? But we both know that even if we don't write much we keep thinking of each other all the time.

Last time I told you about how our *kibbutz* started. This time I must tell you about the other members. They are all fine people and sometimes I find it hard to live up to their standards. The other girls are Sue, ' Piggy ' and Denise. Sue and Piggy work together in a young people's boutique. Sue is very lively and pretty and worries about the size of her bust !—but actually it's only 39 inches, just 3 more than my own. Piggy is quite pretty too (though she doesn't think so herself) but sometimes she is more reserved than Sue. I think perhaps both of them have not had very happy lives at home in the past but are now enjoying themselves very much. It must be dreadful to have an unhappy home but that is something I wouldn't know about. Then there is Denise. Denise is terrifically pretty and smart. At first you might think she is a bit scatter-brained but you would be making a big mistake. Actually she is very sweet and I can't imagine any man not falling for her head-over-heels at sight.

Sue is very dark, Denise is a redhead and Piggy is somewhere between. I suppose I'm a Swedish silver-blonde so we've got a bit of everything!

And now about our four men, who are called, Ted, Max, Tubby and Willie. Ted has a beard, Max is the best looking one, Tubby is plump and cherubic (I mean cherubic in appearance, not really in behaviour). They are all very cheeky but behind the cheek there is a lot of chivalry. I think that Mom, whom I have always looked upon as a pretty sound man-picker, would approve of our quartette.

She might not, I suppose, entirely approve of all our domestic arrangements, which get a bit mixed up at times. Still, on second thoughts, I think she would. You see, I am very happy and as you have both said so often, if one is really happy there cannot be very much wrong with one's way of life.

I have got over the disappointment of my ballet career not working out. But really I started much too late and the bones of my toes, having got past the stage when they could be shaped and developed by the exercises, would never have become strong enough to let me use my points. Fancy a ballerina who couldn't stand on her points! Still, the little training I did helps me to enjoy and appreciate ballet performances more than ever.

On reading back, I find I omitted to say anything

about Willie when mentioning the others. Well, Willie is quite nice but a bit of a worry to us all, because he is trying to be an author but cannot find plots. He is not very good-looking because he has a bent nose which he got broken in a boxing class at school. I'm very stupid because now I've made him sound like a roughneck, which he is really nothing like at all.

Oh, did I ever tell you that they think here I am of Russian descent! It's a good joke and I'm seeing how long I can keep it up.

Well, I think that's about all for now. My job in the solicitor's office suits me fine and I still like London and will probably spend the rest of my life here. Also, I don't think I'll ever get married—but, as you have always said, what I do with my life is my own affair, provided only that the graph keeps going upwards and never down. I long to see you both again and must manage it somehow before too long. I don't suppose Mom's arthritis makes it very easy for her to take a quick trip back to England before your term is up—though if you could both manage it I'd love the other *kibbutzers* to meet you, and we'd manage somehow to put you up at the *kibbutz*. But failing that I'll just have to save up for a visit to Canada, perhaps next year. In the meantime, please keep well, both of you.

All my love and a hundred kisses to you both.

Olga.

Olga read the letter through. She felt dissatisfied with it, because although she had done her best with it, it still seemed to her cold and impersonal and not nearly so good a letter as her parents deserved. Still, she just didn't have the ability to write a better one, so she sealed it in its envelope and put it in her handbag to post on the way home. She wished she had Willie's gift for writing.

It was a lovely evening. On her way home from business Olga decided to spend a while in Trafalgar Square watching the pigeons before going back to the *kibbutz*. The pigeons amused Olga. She liked the way the hen wandered casually about, pretending to be unaware of the cock strutting lustfully after her. He never seemed to catch up, at least not when the square was thronged with crowds of people. But obviously he must, sometime—perhaps they got together in the small hours before dawn when the square was deserted and even the starlings on their ledges overhead were silent.

She saw then, that Willie Torr was one of the people in the square. He was squatting on his heels, feeding the pigeons from a little paper bag. She was behind him, some ten yards away, and her first instinct was to creep up and blindfold him with her hands. But something stopped her—some feeling of taking a fortuitous advantage of him. There was no obligation for the *kibbutz* men to show an interest in the *kibbutz* women during the hours of daylight. In that they were unlike the pigeons, even if their nocturnal habits had similarities.

She thought, he sees enough of me with this new rota. It took quite an effort to turn away but she was doing it when suddenly Willie swivelled on his heels and looked directly at her, as if he'd had eyes in the back of his head.

With a little joyous gesture he immediately threw the bag up in the air, scattering the seeds and causing a wild flutter of greed among the pigeons. Then he rose and came towards her. He'd changed his clothes since breakfast time and was now all in black—black slacks and black polo-neck sweater—and with his bent nose looked like a boxer out for a training run.

He stopped in front of her and eyed her up and down, his head on one side. Olga too was in black, but with white collar, epaulettes and cuffs, a trim modified-mini frock which went to the sedate limit considered seemly by Sloane, Medway & Sloane. It had little brass balls for buttons all down the front, which gave it a military air that she had thought would gratify Mr. Medway.

Willie's eyes showed appreciation—even if his words didn't.

" You saw me but you were sneaking off," he said in a friendly accusing tone. " Russian swine."

" Oh Willie, don't you see enough of me at the moment—?"

" It must be all of nine hours since I clapped eyes on you. Nine hours of excruciating effort—"

" Feeding pigeons?"

" No—looking for a plot."

" Any luck?"

" Sweet bugger-all, as usual," he said. " Look—let's go somewhere—"

" You mean, for a cup of tea—?"

" No. Let's have a meal and do a show—sort of break out."

She considered. He really did seem glad to see her. She wondered if he could afford it.

" Dutch treat?" she asked.

"Hell no. I'm all right—I haven't spent much this week."

She knew he would be offended if she made an issue of it.

" All right," she said.

" Where'd you like to go?"

She had no difficulty in answering that one. " *The Sleeping Beauty*'s on at the Festival Hall. But it mightn't suit you—"

" Ballet?"

" Yes. We'll go somewhere else if you'd rather—"

" No—ballet's fine. I'll tell you something—I've never seen a full length ballet. If I don't understand it, you'll explain what's going on, won't you?"

" I can try."

" We could have dinner too at the Festival Hall—would you like that?"

" Wouldn't I just," she told him.

" That's settled then," he said. " But let's have a drink first. I'll phone from the pub and book seats and a table."

" Try to get one at the window, looking out on the river," she advised.

" Okay, Sexy, let's go," he said. He put his hands on her shoulders and gave her a formal sort of kiss, his lips touching hers lightly. Then he turned her round and pointed her towards the Strand.

Olga was thinking, how little you know of a man just by sleeping with him. She decided she liked Willie in this new squiring mood. He was showing off a bit, of course—but showing off on account of her. That made her feel good.

104

They went hand in hand down Villiers Street where they sat for half an hour in a pub. During that time they had two drinks, a long and a short one each, and Willie went to the phone. He didn't say anything when he came back and she didn't ask him. She felt he had booked really good seats and wanted to surprise her. He said, " Tell me about *The Sleeping Beauty*. Just in about ten words. So I'll know what to look for."

" Well," she told him, " it's the love story of Princess Aurora and Prince Florimund. An evil fairy puts Aurora to sleep for a hundred years. She can only be awakened by a kiss—"

" And after a hundred years along comes Prince Florimund and he ups and kisses her and they live happily ever after—"

" You know the story—?"

" No—how else could it end? What do I look out for—?"

" Well—there's the Rose Adagio and the dance of the Bluebirds—oh, a hundred other things as well—"

" You'll tell me as we come to them, won't you?"

" You either love ballet or hate it," Olga told him. " If you love it, you won't need to be told. If you hate it, telling wouldn't be any good."

" One thing," Willie said. " Are the men pansies?"

" Some of them are—"

" Do they have to be?"

" To dance well, do you mean? No—they're much better when they aren't. The femininity of the ballerina should be in sharp contrast to the virility of her partner."

" *Vive la différence*—I'm all for that," Willie said. " So much for ballet. Now let's talk about something

D*   105

else. If you were sitting where I am you'd realise how pretty you look. Pretty and mysterious."

Olga almost blushed.

"Oh Willie," she said. "I can't be mysterious to you —you've—well, seen too much of me for that—"

"But you are," Willie insisted. "Women are mysterious to men. So long as the relationship doesn't become humdrum. It's only when they get married that they get bored with each other. I remember my parents, God rest them. They always stayed affectionate towards each other. But there wasn't a pick of mystery left at the end, not a pick, even though they were still quite young when the plane crashed and killed them. They were dear souls. But if they'd separated and each taken a new partner every once in a while it would probably have done both of them a world of good."

"That's good sound *kibbutz* doctrine," Olga said.

It turned out to be a wonderful evening. They had another drink, which Olga insisted on standing, then instead of going by the Hungerford footbridge they strolled hand in hand along the Embankment and across Waterloo Bridge. Dinner was a huge success. Their table for two faced directly out across the river.

Their seats for the ballet were just about perfect too. From Willie's secrecy after making the phone call Olga had expected this, but she stood as if in surprise at the end of the row as the usherette showed them in—stood long enough to utter a grateful "Oh Willie!"

During the performance they held hands down between the seats and Willie sat mute, taking it all in. Olga sensed that he had the soul of a balletomane and didn't need any help or prompting. At the end of the Rose Adagio he simply said, "Who is she—?"

Olga didn't need to ask if he was referring to Princess Aurora.

"Dagmar Kessler," she told him.

"She's good," Willie said, "isn't she? Damnit, she must be good. Maybe as good as they come—?"

"Just about," Olga said. She considered a moment, trying to give a balanced judgement, as she always did about ballet.

When concentrating she had a habit of puckering her eyebrows that gave her an elfin look. Willie liked that look; he sat now just studying it surreptitiously. He thought, there's really no doubt who's the prettiest of the *kibbutz* women. Olga interrupted his study by delivering her judgement. "You know, Willie, today's top ballerinas, including Kessler, are probably all better than Pavlova. The public won't believe it—but it's true. Techniques have improved so much since then."

"I didn't know people could do those things with their bodies," Willie said. "When you were taking ballet lessons could you do things like that?"

Olga had to smile.

"Oh, they were called by the same names—arabesques and pirouettes and *fouettés* and all the rest of it. But they weren't the same. Compared with Kessler I was an elephant with head staggers—on crutches."

He looked at her and grinned.

"Nice elephant."

Olga had been happy all evening but now for some reason she suddenly felt quite enormously happy. It must, she told herself, be because of having someone to share her love of ballet with.

The audience was still applauding the Rose Adagio.

Through the applause Willie caught a scarcely audible whispered conversation which seemed to be taking place between a very small boy and his mother. It was coming from somewhere nearby but he couldn't be sure just where.

The childish voice said, "Oh look, Mummy—there's another ballerina, sitting over there." The older voice asked, "Where?" "There—beside the man with the bent nose. Why isn't she dancing, Mummy?" "She's not a ballerina, darling—at least, I *think* not. She's just a pretty lady in the audience." "But she *must* be a ballerina, Mummy—can I go and ask her?" "No, darling, I'm afraid you can't." "But wouldn't you like to speak to her too, Mummy?" "Yes—but you can't just go up to strange ladies." "But she wouldn't mind, Mummy—I know by looking at her that she wouldn't mind." "Maybe not—but it simply isn't done. Now do be quiet, darling . . ."

Willie was thinking, the little bastard—he called me the man with the bent nose. But suddenly he realised that he wasn't offended at all. He was actually pleased —pleased and proud to be sitting beside Olga. He couldn't believe it was reasonable that a snatch of overheard childish chatter should have that effect on him. Crazy, he thought—but nice crazy. He glanced at Olga but quite obviously she hadn't heard; she had been too busy applauding . . .

Afterwards, going home in darkness over Waterloo Bridge, Willie suddenly took Olga in his arms and kissed her. He achieved the considerable feat of being gentle about it and at the same time wildly erotic and stimulating. He had never kissed her quite like that before. She was conscious of her knees wobbling under her. It puzzled her that the most successful kiss they had ever exchanged should happen standing up on Waterloo Bridge.

"Golly," she said breathlessly when he finally released her, "you really meant that one, didn't you?"

He grinned at her in the reflection from the riverside lights. Even his grin was different—there was a lot more in it than just an ordinary grin. His bent nose made him look like a slightly-flawed faun. Olga suspected that *his* knees had wobbled a bit too. He waved a hand airily.

"It's just part of the Willie Torr service. Anytime, anytime."

"Oh Willie, thanks for a wonderful evening—"

He seemed almost embarrassed by her thanks and to hide his embarrassment simulated a comical indignation.

"What d'you mean, evening? God, don't tell me you've forgotten this is only the day-shift. We've got till breakfast time."

She laughed and linked her arm in his, pulling him towards the Embankment. "No, I haven't forgotten, Willie—come on, let's go home."

By an extraordinary and totally unforeseen coincidence, a fortnight later and almost on the same day, Olga and Piggy, unknown to each other, found that something that should have happened hadn't happened.

They checked with calendars and looked up the little cryptic code-marks they had made in their diaries, hoping they had made a miscalculation. But they hadn't. So they uneasily waited a little longer, hoping against hope. But still nothing happened. Finally there could be no reasonable doubt about it.

They were both pregnant.

FIVE

OLGA AND Piggy differed completely in their reaction to their pregnancies.

Olga decided to tell the other *kibbutzers* at once. She felt that, all things considered, they had a right to know. Piggy, on the other hand, determined to keep her condition a secret as long as possible. Perhaps this was because of her family background. She had been less accustomed than Olga to sharing her problems with other people, particularly her parents.

Piggy just couldn't visualise a tolerable existence for herself outside the *kibbutz*. Being a Farthingale, if she tried to organise her life on her own, she'd only end up in a sordid psychological pigsty as Fred and Vicky had done. Not to end up like Fred and Vicky was the one great lesson life had taught her. She knew what Vicky would have done with an unwanted child—had an abortion (or rather a terminated pregnancy as they called it nowadays). Everyone did it these days. They came to London from all over the world to have it done. In the end she'd probably join the queue. She'd have no difficulty paying for the best attention—she still had the £1,500 left her by Fred. Also, she supposed, that

111

would be the solution which would best suit the *kibbutz* and cause it the least disturbance. But there was no immediate hurry. She must think and think and think again before she did anything drastic.

And in the meantime she'd tell no one. Not even Max. Even in her inmost heart she didn't blame Max for what had happened. The responsibility was hers—she must have been worrying so much about Fred's death that she'd forgotten her drill.

Olga took a different view of what was due to the *kibbutz*. In the later stages a pregnant woman flopping about the house wouldn't be much of an asset. They'd be sure to want her to go so that they could get someone else in her place to keep the balance of numbers. That would be too bad for her personally but would be perfectly reasonable and understandable. The plain fact was that it had been originally agreed that when any member of the *kibbutz* ran into a difficulty that in any way affected the rest, it would be better to discuss it with the other members at a full meeting called for the purpose. Pregnancy definitely came under the heading of a difficulty.

Neither girl blamed anyone but herself. Olga wasn't going to natter at Willie about it any more than Piggy would natter at Max. None of them were exactly innocents and all the girls had chosen the life of the *kibbutz* voluntarily, knowing the implications and possibilities.

At breakfast on the day after she was certain of her condition Olga said, during a lull in the conversation, " Oh by the way, everyone—I'm pregnant."

They all froze and stared at her. Some had their cups or their forks half way to their mouths; they just stayed that way, as if the music had stopped in a nursery game. Willie was the only exception. He dropped his spoon with a clatter and choked on his cornflakes. Olga didn't look directly at anyone but she could sense all their reactions. She'd known Willie would be shocked but this had seemed as kind a way to break it to him as any. In a symbolic sort of way it lifted the weight from him and shared it among everybody. Poor Willie. He must be feeling that the world had altered course since they were in bed together half an hour ago.

But she noticed also that Piggy's reaction was almost as marked as Willie's. That surprised her—she couldn't imagine why Piggy should show so much more astonishment than the other five.

Tubby was the first to dissolve the still-life tableau.

" Preggers?—good show," he said at last, grinning.

" It's not a good show at all," Olga said. " But I thought I'd better tell you all."

Sue said quickly, " It'll be all right, Olga. You don't have to worry about a thing. Only whatever you do, don't let it break up the *kibbutz*. I mean—your baby's important of course but the *kibbutz* is damned important too—"

Denise said reassuringly, " It's happened before, you know. Even Homer nodded—"

" He may have nodded," Olga said. " But I'd be surprised if he got pregnant." She felt it would help Willie to get over his shock if she treated it lightly.

Apart from Tubby none of the men had said anything. She hoped Willie would continue for the moment not to say anything. He didn't look fit to speak—he looked as if someone had clubbed him. Anyway, what could men usefully say about pregnancy—?

Piggy asked quietly, "What are you going to do, Olga? Are you going to have it—?"

Olga made an indeterminate gesture.

"I—I've hardly thought about it yet. I wasn't even sure till yesterday. It's still nearly as much of a surprise to me as to the rest of you—"

"That's right—give her time," Sue said.

Olga was still hoping Willie wouldn't speak yet. Coming suddenly like this, Willie—being Willie—would have a sense of guilt. If he spoke now he would probably blurt out an offer of marriage. That wouldn't do—it simply wouldn't do at all.

Denise said, "Why don't we all think about it for a day or two? How we can help, I mean. Then we could have a proper *kibbutz* discussion. Unless Olga doesn't want that—"

"I'd like it," Olga said.

There were murmurs of agreement all round. Olga suddenly felt relief at having got her announcement over. They had taken it very well. She hoped now someone would get up and go and then she could follow quickly. If they didn't they'd all be late for work. Most of all, she didn't want to talk to Willie just yet. It would be too easy to lead Willie into a trap from which we would never escape—that musn't happen, whatever else did.

To her relief Tubby pushed back his chair and rose.

"Well, that's settled then," he said cheerfully. "We'll all think about it for a while and then have a pow-wow. In the meantime, don't take any wooden nickels."

He bustled off to his launderettes. Everyone else had risen too. Olga saw Willie moving towards her. She

114

gave him a quick smile, pretending not to realise that he wanted to talk to her. She joined Sue and Denise and Piggy as they went out into the hall. She had purposely left the small articles she needed for the day on the hallstand, so that she could pick them up and walk straight out to the street.

" Cheerio," she called. " I'm late—got to hurry."

As she swayed, strap-hanging, along the Metropolitan line on her way to the offices of Sloane, Medway & Sloane, she reflected, not long ago I was telling myself life would run smoothly on unchanged until I began to get old and only then would I have to make other arrangements. Well, she'd certainly got her timetable wrong. Now she'd have to get down to a really big think.

At the moment she half-glimpsed herself in one of two possible situations. One was bringing up a child by herself in a bed-sitter somewhere in London. Hardly hilarious—but lots of girls did it and at least they didn't let you starve nowadays. The other was going to her parents' home in Canada with a baby in her arms. Her parents would certainly take her in and make much of her and her baby. But really, the more she thought about it the more she felt it simply wasn't on. One of her theories about living your own life was that when you got yourself into a scrape you somehow got yourself out of it again—unaided. It was no use just having rules when things were going for you. You weren't much use if you couldn't stick to them when the going turned a little rough. And it certainly wasn't a time for tears and emotional upheaval.

There were other possibilities too, of course—but most of them didn't look as if they'd stand up to a cool calm appraisal. The really vital thing was to make sure that Willie didn't get bogged down with her worries. Life held more important things in store for Willie than that.

Olga didn't regard it as at all odd she should think in this way. It seemed to her merely common sense to arrange the affairs of life in order of importance. Once she had decided on a certain order she rarely found it necessary to chop and change or mess about with it. She wasn't sure whether this was a good or bad thing but in any case she couldn't help it—it was just the way she was made.

That evening Ted, Max and Tubby went to a billiards hall to play three-handed snooker. They were also going to discuss Olga's pregnancy. They didn't invite Willie along because they took it for granted that he, as Olga's room-sharer, was responsible for her condition and so could hardly be expected to be impartial.

Tubby didn't really want to discuss Olga. He realised that in order to compensate for his queer awe complex he would take sides against her. As he was going into the billiards hall he knew he would talk like Judas Iscariot no matter how he tried to fight against it.

He chalked his cue and broke off, just touching the nearest right-hand red of the pyramid and coming back into balk. As they carried on from there, the three of them chatted quietly so that the users of neighbouring tables wouldn't hear.

" It was certainly a bit of bad luck," Max said.

" She must have forgotten to take her pill or something," Tubby observed. " In future before we make love we'd better ask them if they've done their drill."

" Don't be so bloody crude," Ted said. " They're nice girls. You can't treat them like that. You're not a flight captain ticking off the things his crew must do before he can get airborne."

" I still think it was damned carelessness," Tubby said (opposition always made him worse). " It's letting the *kibbutz* down. No matter what she decides to do, she's bound to be out of circulation for a while—"

Max suddenly mis-cued; his face was becoming red with anger.

"Fat swine," he said, forgetting to keep his voice down. " They're all nice girls but Olga's the nicest of the lot. Now she's had the rotten luck to get knocked up all you can think of is your own selfish pleasure." His face was really blazing now; he caught Tubby by a lapel. " Pregnant by another man or not, I'd marry her tomorrow if she'd have me—"

"More fool you, then," Tubby said. " Take your bloody hands off me—"

Players at neighbouring tables were beginning to look towards them. Tubby and Max were shaping up to each other; Ted, who had been sighting a red, his beard rubbing against the cue, straightened up quickly and pushed them apart.

" For God's sake have a bit of bloody sense, you two —we don't want to get thrown out—"

They calmed down with ill grace and Tubby smoothed out his lapel where Max had crumpled it.

" I get riled when someone talks a lot of crap at me," he said. " ' If she'd have him,' he says. Of course Olga would have any of the four of us right now—it would be a good let-out for her and nobody could blame her—"

"Stupid fat bugger," Max hissed in an undertone. "You know nothing about women like Olga—little dolly tarts are more in your line—"

"You're still talking crap," Tubby snarled. He looked at Ted. "Tell him he's talking crap for God's sake—"

"But he's not," Ted said.

Tubby stared at him.

"Christ, you too—?"

"If Olga ever marries it won't be because some fellow's knocked her up," Ted said. "It'll be because she's re-thought her ideas of freedom. And because she thinks marriage will be good for her man's career. She doesn't think that about any of us at the present, least of all Willie. She believes the wedded state would bugger up any literary inspiration he possesses, which God knows may be little enough. Oh and another thing—they'd have to be God-awfully in love with each other."

Max was looking at Ted with a new sort of respect. "So you know about Olga too? I didn't think you had that much perception."

"You don't need perception. You just need to live with Olga for a while, as we've all done."

"It doesn't seem to have worked that way with our fat friend, then," Max said drily.

"Don't be too sure—you don't have to take everything Tubby says at its face value. It's not easy to think straight about Olga. She's not a standard model —she's a special job."

Tubby was staring from one to the other.

"You're mad," he said. "You're both idealistic lunatics. This isn't a bloody séance. And women aren't like that—"

"Olga is," Max said.

" Well, chase my Aunt Fanny round the gasworks,"
Tubby said to the room in general.

Suddenly the snooker game had gone sour. They stood
facing each other, their hands clasping their cues and
the butts resting on the floor, like soldiers ceremonially
guarding a bier.

" Oh hell," Tubby said, " You two rotten bastards are
ganging up on me. Let's go and have a drink somewhere."

They put the cues back in the rack, settled with the
attendant and moved towards the exit. All three had
their hands deep in their pockets and looked and felt
disgruntled. They had never quarrelled to this extent
before.

Tubby was thinking, what a terrible thing it is to
be in awe of somebody. It's a sort of slavery—it makes
you talk out of the top of your head. You opened your
mouth and what came out was the exact opposite of
what was inside. He wondered if it affected everyone this
way or was he some sort of nut?

At the boutique, in the intervals between serving
customers, Sue and Piggy, too, were discussing Olga's
pregnancy.

" I always had the feeling at the back of my mind
that one of us *kibbutz* girls might boob sooner or later,"
Sue said. " Doing it so steady, I mean. Didn't you?"

" Honestly, no," said Piggy. " I thought it was almost
foolproof nowadays. Of course it was stupid of me—
but it just never occurred to me as a serious risk." (She
added inwardly, not until it happened to myself.)

" There's always a risk when there's a human ele-
ment—"

"In this case it's all human, isn't it?—they haven't invented any machinery yet that's as good—"

"You know what I mean. And sooner or later there are bound to be more slip-ups."

Piggy thought, you'd be surprised if you knew how soon. But she only said, "Thank God it's not like the days when you had to go jump in the river."

"The rivers would be jammed with bodies," Sue said. "Not a river anywhere would be navigable."

"Nowadays nobody blinks an eye when you say, 'I'm Miss Bloggs and this is my little daughter.' Well —hardly anyone."

Sue giggled.

"At least we're pretty sure who the father is. We're not like the two women who were admiring each other's babies. One said, 'Your little boy's got nice curly hair—did his father have curly hair?' And the other said, 'Dunno—he didn't take his hat off '."

Piggy failed to laugh. She said. "They've still got to be brought up."

"Unless one gets rid of them."

"I'm sure Olga won't do that."

"So am I," Sue said. "Do you think she'll get married?"

"I don't know," Piggy said.

"She couldn't very well stay on at the *kibbutz* if she did, could she?" Sue said. "I mean, you can't have a married couple mixed in with the rest of us. It would be the thin end of the wedge—the beginning of the end of the partner-changing system. It just wouldn't be decent."

"What will she do then? Go away?"

"We none of us want her to go away either.

She's a pretty swell *kibbutzer*. I've been thinking."

"You've got a plan, haven't you?" Piggy said. She had felt all along that Sue was working on something.

"Yes. Why doesn't the *kibbutz* set up a nursery of its own?"

"My God—you *have* been thinking."

"There's the whole top floor of 32 Roxton Gate lying unused." Sue said. Piggy could see that this was the something Sue had been working on and that she was bubbling with enthusiasm inside. "We could get someone in full-time to look after it—maybe Mrs. Williams would do it. On her times off we girls could take it in turns to look after things. Spread over four it wouldn't be a very demanding chore. And if all eight of us chipped in we'd hardly notice the expense. As time went on maybe there'd be three or four kids in the nursery. Their upbringing and education would be the responsibility of the whole *kibbutz*. I mean, we'd take our duties seriously—we'd really do our best for them. They do that sort of thing in parts of Russia, don't they? So why couldn't we do it here? That top floor could be turned into something terrific—posh play pens and all the latest nursery comforts and gadgets. Well, what do you think of it, Piggy?"

"You've taken my breath away—"

"Oh come on, give a snap opinion—say it's mad or it might work or something—"

"It might work," Piggy said.

Inside she felt excited. If this scheme could be got off the ground it would solve her own problem as well as Olga's.

"It's got to work," Sue said enthusiastically. "Take

our own case—it would suit both of us, Piggy. We don't intend to marry. And you've told us about not wanting ever to go home again. Well, I don't want ever to go home again either. My parents are the most ghastly Bible-thumpers—well meaning, I suppose, but insufferable to live with. They think they've got a private hot line to God Almightly—"

"I haven't any longer a home to go to, not even a Bible-thumping one—"

"So you see, we've just got to keep the *kibbutz* going. We'd never be as well fixed again. Cooking and cleaning and slaving for one man would be boring after this. I may be promiscuous but I like this way of life."

"Me too," Piggy said.

"All right, I'll have a word sometime soon with Mrs. Williams," Sue promised. "Provisionally, of course. In the meantime, keep it under your belt."

Piggy almost said, that's just where I've got it. But instead she said, "I'll back you—you can count on me."

One of the customers came forward then, having chosen something, so they had to leave it there.

Sue had asked Mr. Rottger if it would be all right if she was fifteen minutes late getting to the boutique. So this morning she stayed behind in the *kibbutz* after all the others had gone, including Willie who seemed not to be able to settle down to do any writing these days.

Sue was waiting for Mrs. Williams. When the cleaner came in Sue said, "Oh Mrs. Williams, before you start could I have a word with you?"

"Of course, Miss Bottome," Mrs. Williams said. She looked just a little bit apprehensive, as if she was trying to remember if she had inadvertently neglected one of her duties. "I hope I've done nothing wrong."

"No, no it's nothing like that," Sue said. They sat down together on the hall seat and Mrs. Williams took off her hat. She always wore a hat—you looked like a cleaner if you didn't wear one. Sue went on, "It's just my own idea and may never come to anything. But before I suggest it to the others I'd like your opinion about it."

"Well then," Mrs. Williams said, "let's hear it, dearie."

"I thought maybe we should start a nursery on the top floor—"

"Poor dear, you've got caught," Mrs. Williams said quickly, with a sort of enthusiastic sympathy. "And me thinking nobody ever got caught nowadays, what with these pills and things. Well, don't worry, dearie, you're not the first. In my day we liked our bit of nookie too but the numbers as got caught was something awful—"

As soon as she could get a word in, Sue said, "No, no—I'm not pregnant—"

"Then one of the other young ladies is—"

"There's nothing absolutely certain yet, Mrs. Williams—but accidents happen, we all know that," Sue said. "It's—it's really a sort of provision for the future. What I wanted to ask is, if we started a nursery on the top floor would you like to take charge of it?"

"Me?" Mrs. Williams said. The offer came as a delightful surprise to her. She wondered if it could possibly mean moving into 32—she'd love that because she was getting tired of living alone. "I'm good with children—I reared six of my own, all married and gone away now."

"It would be full-time. You'd live in and have your own room beside the nursery—and your keep, of course. We might even manage a television for you too, later on. You'd really be a sort of nanny—"

"Me a nanny," Mrs. Williams said, chuckling. She was old enough to remember when superior young persons dressed like nurses had pushed prams round the square and turned up their noses at lesser servants.

"You'd have your times off, of course—"

"I wouldn't want off much—pushing a pram round the square would be nearly enough—"

"No—you'd want more than that," Sue said. "One of us girls would stand in for you, of course. We wouldn't be able to pay you a lot—"

"You wouldn't need to," Mrs. Williams said. "I've got my pension. A pound or two a week on top of that, with my food and board—I'd be on the pig's back—"

"We might manage more than a pound or two— maybe as much as four. When the baby's asleep maybe you could continue to do a little cleaning too. Of course, we'd help with that more than we do now—"

"You've got it all thought out, haven't you?" Mrs. Williams said admiringly.

"Yes—but it may never happen, don't forget," Sue said. "I'd have to get the approval of the others. But before I suggest it to them I wanted to know if you'd take it on."

"Yes—I'd take it on flying," Mrs. Williams said eagerly. "I just hope it comes to pass, that's all."

"Good." Sue said. "Well, I've got to rush to work now. You will keep it under your hat, won't you, Mrs. Williams? You see, it'll be nearly nine months before anything much happens, in any case—"

"Oh?" Mrs. Williams said, a little disappointed. "I thought maybe it was beginning to show. It could be just a false alarm, couldn't it—? I remember once I could have sworn—"

"I don't think so," Sue said. "But the—the mother mayn't even want to have it in the *kibbutz* at all. So please don't count on it—and please, please keep it under your hat. I'll tell you when there's anything definite. And now I really must be going."

"I'll keep my fingers crossed," Mrs. Williams said.

At the hall door Sue paused and stood sideways. "By the way, I'm trying a new type of bra," she said. "Does it do anything for me?"

Mrs. Williams cocked her head on one side and eyed Sue critically (she knew about Sue's big-bust complex).

"You look right neat, Miss Bottome," she said. "You don't want to get too flat. Men like to have something to get a grip on."

As Mrs. Williams did her cleaning that morning she kept humming, 'Roll me over in the clover'. She hoped fervently it wouldn't prove to be a false alarm. She wondered which of the young ladies it was. Could be any of them—they were all hard at it, bless 'em.

She thought then, Oh Gawd, how lovely it would be to be young again.

Willie gave a sort of little strangled moan.

"But why—*why* won't you marry me? I still don't understand."

"I've told you—every night for ages," Olga said. "It wouldn't be good for you."

"You don't love me—you don't even like me."

"Willie dear, I—I like you very much."

"But what about the baby? It's my baby too. It'll need a father."

"It'll get along very nicely with its mother. If it's a boy I'll call it Willie."

"Thank you very much for that—that fixes everything," Willie said sarcastically. "You're crazy. The whole world's crazy."

They were in bed. The rest of the *kibbutz* had gone to sleep long since. The summer night outside and the phosphorescence that always hung over London turned the windows (if you used your imagination) into pale mother-of-pearl casements that might just as easily have looked out on coral islands and moonlit lagoons as on a rather seedy square. They had been arguing like this for hours. Indeed for many nights now bed had turned into a sort of forum for controversy.

"We'd better go to sleep," Olga said, "or we'll look like nothing in the morning. The others'll think we've been quarrelling all night—"

"We have been," Willie said. "They'll be bloody well right."

"No—we've been discussing."

"Discuss some more then. Tell me again why you won't marry me. If you repeat it often enough maybe I'll even begin to see a glimmer of sense in it."

"Oh Willie, you are a nuisance," Olga said. "Well, first of all, there's the *kibbutz* angle. You know what it stands for—complete freedom, no ties. We came into it voluntarily. It would be like a—a nun or a monk going back on their vows—"

"Christ, what a comparison—"

"Secondly, what happened was my fault. I got careless. I see no reason why you should be held responsible—"

"Crap," Willie said. "Complete and utter crap so far—and you know it. Now tell me the real reason. You don't love me, isn't that it—?"

"No-o—not really—"

Willie snorted in the half darkness.

"Oh you like me well enough to make love to, I know that. But not well enough to spend the rest of your life with—just the two of us, I mean. There's a hell of a difference. Let me tell you something. I like making love to the other three girls—in fact I like it very much because I'm human. But for months past I've found myself longing for the rota to come round and bring you and me together again. You remember the afternoon you came back early?—your boss was playing golf or something. I was sharing with Piggy at the time. Piggy's fine—and physically satisfying. Yet you know what happened—"

"Let's—let's not pretend," Olga said. "I knew you were feeling—well, randy. You'd been sitting over a typewriter all day. I was sorry for you. And there was nothing in the rules against what we did—"

"God, I thought you understood," Willie said. "There was so much more to it than just that." He lay staring at the dark ceiling and she could sense the bitterness in him. "You don't know what love is, Olga, that's the real trouble."

She didn't answer for quite a long time because she had to wait until her voice would be steady. Then she said quietly, "Maybe I don't, Willie."

"Too bloody straight you don't."

"Anyway there are other important things besides

127

love. There's what a man does with his life when he's not in bed. You could be a good writer, Willie—I still think you will be, one day. But not if you burden yourself with a wife and family before you're in a position to keep them, Willie. That way the most you'd ever achieve would be to turn out pulp rubbish fast enough to keep yourself and your dependants just above the starvation level. You deserve better than that, Willie."

"You see," he said, "you really don't understand about love. Behind it all there's this mercenary outlook—"

"Now it's you who don't understand," Olga said.

He turned on his side towards her and in the dim light she could see his eyes staring at her. She could also see his nose, his lovely bent nose that always aroused her motherly and more-than-motherly instincts. She thought, if he makes love to me now, so help me I'll marry him and we'll spend the rest of our lives in the modern equivalent of a garret and we'll be happy enough in our own way. But the name of Willie Torr will never appear in the anthologies and although I'll do my level best for him I'll never quite be able to forgive myself for that.

But suddenly Willie said, "Oh Christ!" and turned his back on her. Finally they went to sleep back to back which was most unusual for them.

A few evenings later everyone arranged to be in for dinner and the whole *kibbutz* sat in to discuss Olga's pregnancy in a sort of benevolent advisory capacity. Sue was elected leader of the discussion which was held as they sat on at table after dinner. She sat with her arms folded on the table, a habit she'd got into to hide her top measurement.

"Of course any final decision can only be made by Willie and Olga," she said. "The rest of us are just background helpers like—well, like the nurse in Romeo and Juliet—"

"Only not so coarse," Denise said.

"God, I hope it'll end better than Romeo and Juliet," Ted remarked.

"It was only an illustration—you know what I mean," Sue said. "But first let's hear if Willie and Olga have decided on anything."

Willie seemed to be disgruntled—as he had been for days now. When he was in this mood his bent nose gave him a sort of tragic look. "I've said all I have to say— to Olga," he told them. "It wasn't any bloody good."

Sue kept eyeing him for a moment or two hoping he would elaborate a bit on that. But she saw he wasn't going to so she turned towards Olga.

"Olga?"

"I—I'd like to hear what advice you all have to offer first," Olga said.

"Well then, the discussion's thrown open," Sue announced.

Tubby said, "My personal advice, for what it's worth would be to get rid of it—"

"Beautifully put," Ted remarked acidly. He gave his beard a tug as if trying to pull it off; with Ted that indicated irritation.

"What's wrong with what I said?" Tubby asked in an aggrieved voice. "We want to be practical, don't we? I have a friend who got it done. She says there's nothing to it nowadays, it's just a bit pricey, that's all. I was going to say that I'd be happy to subscribe towards the cost of the operation. I'm sure the rest of you would too. It's like when somebody scores an own goal, all the team rally round and play harder to make up for it—"

"A beautiful simile," Ted said again, "apt and delicate. Really beautiful."

"Christ," Tubby said. "I'm only trying to help."

"Just a moment," Sue interrupted. "Olga may want to come in on this—"

"I won't have an abortion," Olga said quietly. "I'm sorry, but whatever happens I won't have that."

"I knew she'd say that," Max exclaimed, looking round the table. "She's perfectly right, of course. Abortion's a sort of legalised murder, isn't it—?"

Denise said matter-of-factly, "I don't think I quite agree. What's the use of all these advances in medical services and science if we don't make use of them? It's up to every woman to decide whether or not she wants a baby. If she doesn't, that shouldn't mean she can't have any sex life. All right, she has a sex life and because of carelessness or for some other reason she gets caught. So she has an abortion under good clinical conditions. I can't see what's wrong with that. Of course only the woman herself can make the final decision. She may be guided by what the father says but the last word must be hers. In this case Olga's made her decision. So let's stop talking about abortion and get down to seeing if we can help Olga have her baby in comfort." She added, "And in a way that doesn't harm the *kibbutz*."

Willie had been sitting with bowed head, just as he sometimes did when he was searching for a plot. He raised it now and his bent nose looked more bent than ever. "We could of course get married—if you'll pardon the expression," he said.

They all turned and looked at him as if he'd said something original or eccentric.

Olga said quickly, "Please, Willie. We've discussed that and you know I don't want to get married."

Willie shrugged.

"I know," he said. "I just thought I'd make my contribution no matter how bloody ridiculous it was. I hope nobody minds. There's got to be a joker in every pack. Just forget I ever said it and carry on where you were. I'm only the father."

So everybody looked away again. Willie wasn't very good at sarcasm.

"Well then, abortion and marriage seem to be out," Sue said. "We're getting somewhere." She looked at Piggy. "Piggy hasn't said anything yet—"

"I've nothing to say," Piggy replied. "You know me. I'm easy. I fall in with the majority."

The discussion seemed to run out of impetus for a moment. Sue was still sitting with her arms folded. She took a deep breath and launched the scheme that had filled her mind so much of late.

"I've got an idea. Why not start our own nursery in the *kibbutz*? There's plenty of room for one up on the top floor."

There was a much longer pause while the novelty of this new suggestion sank in. Sue had realised that at first sight they'd probably consider it too formidable to be practicable. It had seemed like that to herself when it first entered her head. But the more she had thought about it the more feasible it became.

"Christ, a baby farm?" Tubby said. "I don't go much for that sort of thing—"

"Hold your horses," Sue said. "It wouldn't be a baby farm. You make it sound like a stud. We wouldn't deliberately set out to stock it or anything like that. I wouldn't have thought that needed saying. When you take out an insurance policy you don't intend to go straight out and have a crash. Our nursery would be like an insurance policy—it would just be there if it were needed."

"It'd be the first step towards turning the *kibbutz* into a matriarchal society—"

"Try not to be so bloody stupid," Max said in quite a friendly way to Tubby. "It's the women who bear the children—to that extent all societies are matriarchal, aren't they?"

He waited for Tubby's comeback but Tubby only grunted. Tubby had a keen business instinct and the idea of insuring against this particular risk was beginning to appeal to him. Sue suddenly felt that the meeting was coming round.

"Olga's case has shown us how easily accidents can happen," she urged. "How can we be sure there won't be any more? Anyway, there'd be at least one baby in our nursery. So it wouldn't be a white elephant or Sue Bottome's Folly or anything like that."

"It would take a lot of planning," Denise pointed out. "For one thing, who'd look after it—?"

"Oh we'd find someone," Sue said airily. "Maybe Mrs. Williams would do it. We'd have to fit it up properly, of course—we want to do the little beggar proud. There'd be the baby's room and the nanny's room and a bathroom and things. But it shouldn't be too expensive, spread over all of us. We could regard it as the premium on our insurance policy. Needless to say the mother would have complete control over the up-bringing of her own child but the rest of us would all be sort of honorary godparents. It might turn out to be a lot of fun. I can even see Tubby constantly dashing up-stairs to tickle it under the chin."

"That's all very well and maybe I would," Tubby said. "But there are a lot of other issues involved—for instance, would Olga still carry out her—er—duties as a loyal *kibbutzer?* I mean, she wouldn't become a one-man woman or anything *bourgeoise* like that, would she—?"

"I see no reason why she should," Sue said. She looked at Olga. "You'd better ask her."

"All right, Olga, I'm asking you," Tubby said.

Olga sat thinking for a long time before she answered.

"I—I just don't know yet, Tubby. I don't know yet what the side-effects of having a baby are. It does things to you—I can tell you that already. On top of it there's this nursery idea—two new things at once. I'd have to think it over before I could give an honest answer."

"Fair enough," Tubby said. "Take your time, Olga —we won't rush you."

"So far so good," Sue said. "She's got months yet. Shall we leave it there in the meantime?" She looked at Piggy again, pointedly this time. "Or has anyone else any observations?" She was remembering that Piggy had promised to back her up.

"Personally I think it's a good idea," Piggy said. "Supposing our luck ran out and we all started having babies like mad—I mean if we became pill-resistant or something. It would be a godsend then, wouldn't it? Instead of each of us having to dash round like crazy making our own arrangements we'd have this nursery ready-made on the premises. In cold money terms we could all have our babies for the price of one, almost. Yes I'm definitely in favour. Put my name down, ma'am."

Ted Allard hadn't said much so far. He'd just sat there in one of his more serious moods, fiddling with his beard and listening.

"Look," he said now, "I'd like to say a couple of things before we adjourn. Anyone listening to us might think we were organising a kip or something. It's not really like that. We're just a bunch of young people who want to live our lives in a way we consider civilised, without interfering with those who think differently, or being interfered with by them. Now a routine problem has cropped up and we're trying to deal with it collectively in a sensible fashion. It's as simple as that. That's one point. The other is, I'd like Olga to know we're all on her side. People talk about happy events —well, when she has her baby we hope it'll really be a happy event for her." He added as an afterthought, "That goes for Willie too, of course."

"Hear, hear," everybody murmured. Somebody raised a cheer.

"Thanks," Willie said without enthusiasm.

Olga was touched. "Thanks from me too—to Ted and everybody. I always meant to have my baby in a way that would be least disrupting to the *kibbutz*. I was beginning to think it would mean going away to live in a bed-sitter by myself. Now there's this other possibility. No matter how positive you were about things beforehand, when you start a baby, you—well, everything's different. Before, you'd just yourself to think about. Now there are, or will be, two other people as well —both awfully important. And at the back of it all there's the *kibbutz*. It takes a bit of re-thinking—being fair to everyone, I mean. Well, I'll do my re-thinking as quickly as possible and let you know. Oh God, I sound like the Lord Chief Justice—"

" I thought you sounded very nice," Sue said. " A bit mixed up but very nice." She looked round the table. " Well, I suppose that's as far as we can take it at the moment."

Everybody nodded. After a moment or two they rose and began to wander off. Piggy was thinking, if Olga's mixed up what am I? She hoped that whatever Olga did, it would help her to make up her own mind—but she doubted it. On a sudden impulse she decided to do a little research on her own.

She buttonholed Max, her room-sharer, on his way out. " Now that we're on the subject," she said casually, " tell me, Max, supposing—just supposing of course— you were to put me in the family way, would you want to marry me?"

" God Almighty," Max said, startled, " what put that into your head—?"

" Oh, just all this talk about a nursery."

He looked relieved.

" You had me worried for a moment—you should give notice of questions like that, you should really." He touched the back of a chair. " Touch wood—lightning doesn't strike the same house twice. Well now, let's see." He stood for a moment considering. If it had been Olga, he admitted to himself, he'd have welcomed the chance —only she wouldn't have him any more than she'd have Willie. But Piggy?—no, he wouldn't want to marry

Piggy, much as he liked her and enjoyed making love to her. He wondered how he could parry her question without telling lies and without hurting her. "We'd have to be loyal to the *kibbutz*, wouldn't we?" he said. "I think we'd have to pop it in the nursery."

"I agree," Piggy said. "It was only a bloody silly academic question, anyway."

SIX

It was odd, but for a day or two after Olga had announced her pregnancy the spirit of the *kibbutz*, for the first time since its inception, had seemed to flag a bit. It was almost as if the players in a poker-school had discovered one of their members, if not actually cheating, at least stretching the rules somewhat.

Then, when Sue made her suggestion about the nursery, everybody had perked up again because it was like looking up the rule-book and finding that the suspect player hadn't cheated at all, that there was actually a provision in the rules for what had at first sight seemed an irregularity.

After that while they waited for Olga to make her decision—which nobody really doubted would be in favour of the nursery scheme—five *kibbutz* members out of the eight practically forgot that such a thing as pregnancy existed. The other three—Olga, Willie and Piggy—thought about it all the time. Olga simply couldn't make up her mind about the nursery, Willie was unhappy because he considered his rights as a prospective father were being ignored by everybody, while Piggy kept wondering how the *kibbutz* would take an-

E*   137

other pregnancy announcement so soon after the first.

The Olga-Willie room-sharing partnership naturally suffered the most strain, mainly because of Willie's touchiness. But Max and Piggy too were beginning to lose a little of their normal good-comradeship. In their case it was due to Piggy's new habit of snapping at Max (who of course knew nothing as yet of her pregnancy) over little things that wouldn't normally have annoyed her. The other two combinations—Sue and Tubby, Denise and Ted—sailed happily on, apparently unaffected.

Mrs. Williams kept mum—and a hopeful eye on all the girls' waistlines.

One evening Piggy and Olga happened to be the only two in the *kibbutz*. Piggy was washing a few smalls and Olga had got out the ironing board and was ironing a pair of Willie's trousers which she had noticed needed it. Willie usually wore jeans that didn't need ironing, but these were his best pair of trousers and some day he'd want them in a hurry and find they were all crushed—which was why Olga was doing them now. Piggy was in the scullery and Olga in the kitchen and they were chatting to each other through the open door between. Piggy still hadn't told anyone about her own pregnancy and didn't intend to until she was at least two months gone and/or beginning to get a tummy.

She asked, " Have you decided anything about your baby yet?"

" Not really—except to have it," Olga said.

" You haven't changed your mind about not having an abortion, then?"

There was a pause and then Olga said quietly, " No—

138

I'll be proud to have Willie's child." She added hurriedly, " I mean, it really was an accident but now it's happened I'm almost glad. When you're—" She broke off. " When accidents happen you've just got to tidy things up as best you can afterwards."

In the scullery Piggy paused, her hands deep in detergent, and watched the bubbles change colour and wink and burst. She thought, Olga was going to say ' When you're in love with somebody ' and then she changed it. So Willie wasn't just a bedfellow. Olga's in love with him. That makes two of us. Oh God, why are women such stupid bitches as to think they can sleep around with men without sooner or later falling in love with them? It might—just might—be possible for Denise and Sue to do it, but not for her and Olga.

Piggy suddenly felt like crying. Or throwing things about the scullery. She would have given anything in the world if the child that was starting its life inside her own body had been Willie's instead of Max's. If she'd had a knife in her hand at that moment she felt she could cheerfully have stuck it into Olga. She went to the door of the scullery, letting her arms drip suds and watched Olga ironing. Olga had a little bowl of water on the ironing board and was dampening a cloth and laying it between the iron and Willie's trousers. Her flaxen hair had fallen over one eye and she was a little flushed with the heat of the iron. As Piggy watched, Olga blew out her cheeks and gave a little puff. For that moment she looked somewhat like a small girl, perhaps an exquisite student-ballerina ironing her own ballet dress after a practice class. Nobody could unconsciously combine sophistication and innocence like Olga.

Even Denise couldn't have managed to look just like that. Olga looks like that because that's the way she is inside—an unspoiled innocent perfectly at home in the permissive society, Piggy decided. God knows how she manages it but she does—with complete success. Piggy knew then she could never really harm Olga—she admired Olga too much, even if the admiration was mixed with a dreadful lot of envy.

Olga looked up and saw Piggy standing in the doorway. She put down her iron and gave Piggy a friendly smile.

"Better not let those suds dry on your arms, Piggy—they're bad for the skin."

Piggy said, "Maybe you'll marry Willie after all."

"No," Olga said, "it wouldn't work. Willie's not ready for marriage. It would mean the end of his writing —he'd be so busy trying to provide for me and the baby."

Piggy stared at her. She was thinking of Vicky and how Vicky would have put back her peroxided head and laughed like hell at what Olga had just said.

"Far be it from me to discourage the noble impulse of self-denial," Piggy said drily, "but realism forces me to point out that Willie hasn't really begun to write yet."

"I know—that's what makes it so serious."

"You really mean—you'd let that stop you marrying him?"

"Yes," Olga said simply. "Wouldn't you—?"

"Let's get this straight," Piggy said. "What do you think men are for?"

"It's more a question of what marriage is for."

Piggy went on staring so hard at Olga that Olga got

a little embarrassed and picked up the iron and bent again over the trousers—Willie's trousers.

"Great God Almighty," Piggy said.

She went back to her washing, shaking her head from side to side and making a clucking noise with her tongue. It could only be the crazy Russian blood, she told herself.

On Sunday, more than a week later, they were all at breakfast. Usually Olga was talkative at breakfast but this morning she was quiet and absorbed. When she was absorbed she frowned slightly and this usually gave her an elfin look; but when uncertainty was mixed with the absorption it somehow added a sulky touch to her expression which was very far from her nature but, according to Ted, made her look terrifically sexy.

He noticed it now and said, "Olga's gone sexy on us. Prepare for a pronouncement."

Olga looked up and smiled at him and then looked round the others.

"I've made up my mind about the nursery," she told them. "I was trying to find the courage to tell you. I—I'm sorry but I don't feel my baby should be the responsibility of the *kibbutz*. It's my baby, not the *kibbutz*'s. I want to look after it on my own."

They stopped eating and focused their attention on her, trying to work out the implications of what she had said. Gradually it dawned on them that this could be the first defection from the *kibbutz*.

"You mean," Sue said quietly, "You're going to leave the *kibbutz*?"

"Yes."

There was silence round the table. The silence, Olga

141

felt, was like herself—pregnant. She heard Willie mutter, "Christ!" She could sense that everyone was sorry. But also she could feel that in some cases disapproval was beginning to mix in with the regret. It was something she had never felt before in the *kibbutz*. It made her feel guilty. She wished they could all read her mind like a book. It was so difficult to explain.

Denise said quietly, "I thought we all felt that loyalty to the *kibbutz* should come before anything else—no matter what."

"I felt that too," Olga said. She found herself picking up a napkin ring and twiddling with it nervously. "But when you start a baby—well, something happens. Not just to your body but to your way of looking at things. I'm not sure my decision is the right one. I've thought about it all the time—honestly I have. I only know that this is what I must do."

They all sat silent again for a while and then Max said, "Oh for God's sake—surely we can think of something so that Olga won't have to leave the *kibbutz*?"

But nobody could. It was obvious from what Olga had said that no compromise was possible.

Piggy asked with an air of casualness, "Is it because you'd feel isolated from the rest of us?—with us but not of us? If there'd been, say two babies due in the nursery instead of just one, would that have made any difference?"

"No," Olga said, "that's really got nothing to do with it. It's no reflection on the *kibbutz* or anyone in it, it's a sort of little compass inside me pointing out the way I must go. I know that sounds just plain stupid. Maybe I am being stupid about it but I can't help myself."

142

" If you leave, it'll mean we've got to find someone else to keep up the numbers," Sue pointed out. " Unless Willie's going too. If he is, we'd have to find two new members."

" Willie won't be leaving," Olga said quickly.

" Mrs. Williams will be terribly disappointed," Sue said. " I may as well tell you all now that I mentioned it to her provisionally and she was dead keen."

For a moment Piggy felt like blurting out that she herself was also pregnant and there would still be need for the nursery. But something held her back. Perhaps she wanted Olga to have left the *kibbutz* before she made her own announcement. Envy did strange things to you. She had no longer any doubt about the reason for her envy—it was because Olga was carrying Willie's child. If I was doing that, she thought, I'd be like Olga—I'd want to go away and keep it to myself. Only of course I'd want Willie to come away with me. When Max's child comes I'll be fond of it too—but somehow it will seem all right to entrust it to the nursery, if there is one.

Tubby's voice cut in on her thoughts. Tubby was saying, " I must say I think it's a bit inconsiderate of Olga not to fall in with the nursery scheme—"

Suddenly Willie shouted, " Stop bullying Olga ! She's made her decision. So shut up, you fat clown !"

They all stared at Willie. It was so unlike him.

" Well, really," Tubby said. " Do you have to be such an unmannerly bloody boor—?"

" Maybe you'd like to teach me manners," Willie said. He made a two-fingered gesture at Tubby.

" Yes, as a matter of fact I would," Tubby said.

He rose and began to take off his coat. Ted, who was

sitting beside him, grabbed his jacket and held it half way down so that Tubby's arms were pinioned. Then he pulled him back into his chair.

"Let me go!" Tubby yelled.

"Oh shut up, the pair of you," Ted said angrily. "You're not in a public bar—or a kindergarden. This is the *kibbutz* and there are ladies present—"

Olga was trying to keep from crying. Poor Willie— gentle Willie! He hadn't even tried to write a word since she had announced her pregnancy. Now he was turning into a quarrelsome fighting man. And all because of her. She wondered how long it would take him to settle when she'd gone.

She got up from the table and ran out of the room and up the stairs. In the bedroom she didn't throw herself on the bed. If she had she knew she'd lie there howling like a stupid schoolgirl until someone came up and tried to quieten her. So she stood at the window and stared out into the square. The shabby square that had known better times. Like herself.

She didn't hear the door open behind her but she felt Willie's arms go round her and his hands find her breasts. He kissed the back of her neck and for a moment she closed her eyes.

"Wherever you go," Willie whispered, "I'm going with you—"

"No," she told him, "no—it wouldn't work out, Willie."

"You don't want me," he said accusingly. He took his arms away suddenly. "You don't love me."

She wanted to deny that with all the vehemence she was capable of. But instead she said, "We've had all this out before—it just wouldn't work."

144

He spun her round and took her in his arms again and kissed her hard on the mouth. She didn't respond —it took a terrific effort but she managed to stay limp. How do you convince a man, she wondered, of a simple thing like this—that you've got to keep out of his life?

Suddenly he held her at arms' length and stared at her. The tilt of his nose, which she had learned to read like a barometer, registered disappointment and chagrin and disbelief. She knew he was remembering Waterloo Bridge.

"Jesus Christ," he said, "you can't even kiss any more."

He turned and went out of the room, slamming the door. He slammed it so hard that the whole *kibbutz* seemed to quiver as if it were on the verge of collapse.

Olga decided not to write and tell her parents about the baby until it actually arrived. Once it was safely in its cot she'd let them know. She knew they wouldn't criticise—they weren't that sort of parents. But if she told them beforehand they'd certainly worry a lot for her and the child. Her mother might even come over in spite of her arthritis, to supervise its arrival.

That left only one person to tell—Mr. Medway. She didn't anticipate undue trouble from Mr. Medway. He had, so far, always been a considerate boss. When he took the afternoon off to play golf he usually let her off too. She wasn't going to ask for much. If need be she'd take the necessary time off as part of her annual leave.

These days Olga was carefully watching the 'apartments vacant' columns in the papers. What she was looking for was a recently married couple who wanted to take in a paying guest. Olga was prepared to pay generously for the right thing. The family must be really nice, kindly people and the mother must be willing to look after Olga's baby by letting it join her own children during the time Olga was at work. Apart from her working hours Olga would devote the rest of her time to her baby. She didn't want it to be under any misapprehension as to who was its real mother. She felt it should be perfectly possible to find such a place. She had plenty of time yet.

In the meantime the important thing was to make sure that her job wouldn't be affected, for she would need the salary for her baby. She decided to tell Mr. Medway on the following morning.

So next morning she waited a little nervously until the buzzer went and Mr. Medway's voice said, " Good morning, Miss Beloff, will you come in please?"

She smoothed down the front of her frock and picked up her notebook and went in. Mr. Medway, as usual, was sitting like the eternal Adjutant, his little moustache looking even more military than usual. She sat down, tucking her short skirt carefully round her thighs. She knew that in ten seconds precisely Mr. Medway would say, ' Take a letter please, Miss Beloff.'

So before he could say that, Olga said, " Just before we begin, I'd like to mention a personal matter, Mr. Medway."

He looked surprised, like an inspecting officer who spies a man in the ranks without a hat, but he said, " Why certainly, Miss Beloff."

" I—I thought it only fair to tell you before you

146

noticed it yourself," Olga said. " In about seven months'
time I'm going to have a baby."

Mr. Medway flinched. He looked now as if he'd seen
that the man in the ranks wasn't only short of a hat
but hadn't any clothes on either.

" A baby—?"

" Yes."

" In seven months—?"

" Yes."

" Good God."

" I'll need a week or two off, of course, but if you
like I could hold part of my annual leave over till then.
I—I just wanted to make sure my job would be open
for me when I came back—"

" But you're not married," Mr. Madway said. " Or are
you—?"

" No, I'm afraid I'm not," Olga said.

" But aren't you going to be married—?"

" No," Olga said. " Does—does it make any difference?"

" Make any difference?" Mr. Medway exclaimed. He
looked absolutely astounded. " *Make any difference?
Great heavens, of course it makes a difference.*" His stare
was so monumentally accusing she had to drop her
eyes.

" I'm sorry," she murmured. There seemed nothing
else to say.

" It's a bit late to be sorry, isn't it?" Mr. Medway
said acidly. " You don't seem to understand. Surely by
now you must know what our clients are like—solid,
substantial, conservative types. What would their reaction be if they suddenly realised we were employing an
unmarried mother?"

" I didn't think they'd even be interested," Olga said. " After all, it's not really their business, is it—?"

"*Not their business?*" (Mr. Medway had an irritating habit of repeating with emphasis anything he didn't agree with.) " Really, Miss Beloff. This firm has been in existence for nearly a century. In all that time it has never employed an unmarried mother—"

" It could begin now, couldn't it?" Olga suggested.

" Is that meant to be impertinent—?"

" No, of course not—"

" It sounded like it, then."

" It really wasn't meant to be." With an unusual flare of anger, Olga was thinking, if there was only myself I'd tell him where to put his job. But she had to think of her baby. So instead she said, " Mr. Medway, whether it's right or wrong, I'm going to have a baby. Bringing up a baby properly is quite expensive. It's important to me that I keep my job. Can't you look at it in that light, please?"

Mr. Medway was tapping his desk with a pencil and frowning now. Mixed up with the frown was a look of distaste, the kind of expression a housewife puts on when she is vacuum-cleaning and finds the dog has done something under the sofa. It suddenly occurred to Olga that this was the sort of thing she'd have to get used to— from certain people. There were more of them left than she'd imagined. Well then, she'd get used to it. For the sake of her baby.

" It's not just the way I look at it, Miss Beloff," Mr. Medway said. " I've got my partners to consider as well."

" Well—couldn't you please consult with them?"

He was still tapping and frowning. Keeping her

in suspense. Suddenly he threw the pencil down.

" I always try to be scrupulously fair," he said at last. He spoke as if he were making a tremendous concession and had doubts if he were justified in doing it. " Even when I find my confidence has been misplaced. I'll lay the matter before my partners at our next official meeting—as you know, we meet weekly. I'll let you know our decision next week, Miss Beloff."

She thought, they have lunch together every day— he could tell me this afternoon if he wanted to.

But she only said, " Thank you, Mr. Medway."

" In the meantime, permit me to dismiss the whole unsavoury episode from my mind. Perhaps you'll be good enough to take that letter now, Miss Beloff."

He had placed a slight but distinct emphasis on the ' Miss '. Olga bent over her notebook. She was beginning to realise how foolish she had been to imagine she could shape her life. From now on it was life that would shape her. She found she couldn't see the paper very clearly because there were tears in her eyes. Up till lately she hadn't cried for years but now it was becoming quite a habit. She stopped herself from doing it now by thinking fiercely, that's exactly what he wants—to make me cry. But I won't—I won't—

Piggie's conscience had been niggling at her—and it was getting worse. She realised it was just possible she might be able to do something for Olga and Willie. But she was making no effort to do it. She wasn't under any delusion as to why she was making no effort. You don't help the fellow you love to get married to someone else—even though you've no chance yourself because you're carrying another person's baby. It was all as complicated as one of those far-fetched clues in a cross-word puzzle.

She got Olga in a corner one evening and began to question her. They had talked a bit about it before but Piggy hadn't been able to make much sense of it. She felt she might do better at a second go. Piggy suspected that Olga and Willie weren't making love any more. For her own satisfaction she'd have liked to question Olga about that but there are limits to what you can pry into.

So instead she asked Olga, "Supposing—just for the sake of argument, mind you—supposing Willie were well-off, would you marry him then?"

Olga shook her fair head quite definitely.

"Not unless he'd plenty of spare time to write."

"Well then, if he were well-off and had plenty of spare time as well, would that make you change your mind?"

Olga considered for a moment but only a moment.

"No—marriage still wouldn't be right for Willie."

"You mean he's not the marrying kind—?"

"No-o. I—I wouldn't altogether say that. It's hard to explain—"

"That's not an overstatement," Piggy said. "But please make the effort—just to satisfy my womanly curiosity."

"Well, even if Willie had money and time, he'd still need a plot. That's been Willie's trouble all along, finding something to write about. Give him that and he'll go on like a house on fire. He's got the ability to keep going only he can't get started—"

"It's a slight drawback," Piggy said.

"Yes. The worst thing is, if he was married he'd never

150

get started. His mind would be so full of making plans for the welfare of his wife and children. Willie's like that. He'll do his duty till he drops. Finding a plot is a lot harder than making money—it's a mental thing, a matter of inspiration. You've simply got to have peace of mind for that. Would Beethoven have composed the Fifth Symphony if he hadn't had peace of mind—?"

"I've heard he was having trouble with his nephew at the time," Piggy said.

"Well, even if he was—maybe his genius worked a different way from Willie's—"

"It's a distinct possibility—"

"Please don't make fun of Willie's genius," Olga said seriously. "Willie *has* got genius—I believe that absolutely—"

"Thousands wouldn't."

"They don't know Willie. If they did, they'd realise that the only important thing—far more important than the *kibbutz* or me or even the baby—is that Willie's genius should get its chance to flower—"

"I wouldn't want to miss that—I love giant sunflowers," Piggy said. "You're usually so sensible. Yet where Willie's concerned you go off your nut. Why don't you just marry the guy and have his baby and let his genius go to hell?"

"That would be no way to treat Willie," Olga said. "You couldn't do it yourself, Piggy."

"Just give me the chance. You're not suggesting Willie might turn you down, are you—?"

"No, I—I don't think he'd do that. But Willie doesn't know what's good for him. He thinks of others too much—"

"And I suppose you don't?"

"Me?" It was obviously a genuinely new thought to Olga. "Heavens no, I'm nothing like Willie in that respect. I'm pretty worldly at heart. I have mean little thoughts no one knows about. You'd be surprised—"

"Oh God." Piggy said. "Why doesn't he clobber you over the head and carry you off like the cavemen did—?"

"No, that's just what Willie wouldn't do. I don't mean he couldn't—he was a boxer at school—I mean he wouldn't. Willie would never force a girl to do what she didn't want to do—"

"Let me batter *my* head against the wall one more time—I think I can survive one more," Piggy said. "If Willie magically came by all three things—money, time and a plot—would you marry him then?"

Olga stared into space with a faraway look.

"I'd certainly consider it," she said. Piggy, watching her closely, saw a sort of light come into her blue eyes for a moment. It faded again almost at once. "But no one can give Willie a plot. That's something he can only do for himself. We've all tried and it was no good. That's the problem."

"It's a proper bugger, isn't it?" Piggy said.

It was almost a week since Olga had broken the news of her pregnancy to Mr. Medway. Today he was due to consult with his partners about her.

After he had dictated his morning letters he went into the elder Mr. Sloane's office for their weekly meeting. Olga didn't remind him that he had promised to bring up the question of her future at the meeting. His attitude these days showed quite clearly he didn't need reminding. He treated her with a subtle lack of respect and constantly made little asides like, 'Nowadays everyone lets one down' and 'Morality seems to be a dirty word these times'. He was ostensibly referring to things in the letters but she knew he meant her to take the asides to herself.

He came back to his own office for half an hour before going off again with his partners for lunch. So he had decided to keep her in suspense as long as possible. It was nearly half past four before his buzzer went.

"I'd like a word with you, Miss Beloff," his voice said coldly. "You needn't bring your notebook in."

She went through to his office. He didn't ask her to sit down so she stood before him—like a private summoned to an Adjutant's Orderly Room for some breach of Queen's Regs. He was fiddling with letters on his desk and didn't look up at her for quite a long time. (It was a trick he had often used in his Army days to soften up the malefactor.)

Then he glanced up and said, "Oh about that matter you mentioned last week."

It wasn't the sort of remark that required an answer but he seemed determined not to go on until she had said something so she murmured, "Yes, Mr. Medway—?"

"I spoke to my partners about it," Mr. Medway said. "I must say they took an extraordinarily lenient view. Not without misgivings, mind you—our primary concern must always be the firm's good name. And not without a sense of having been badly let down. However, their feelings can hardly be of great interest to you, just their decision. Well—after a pretty full discussion we decided not to dismiss you, Miss Beloff."

The way he said all this Olga knew it was a prepared

speech. She wondered if he expected her to thank him effusively. She decided to say nothing but just to turn and go quietly. But he spoke again just as she was turning.

"Just a moment, Miss Beloff. That's not all, of course. Obviously we can't have you dealing directly with our clients when your—er—condition becomes obvious. So you will change places with Miss Hardacre. Miss Hardacre has been studying shorthand in her spare time and, in any case, deserves promotion. It means of course a slight demotion for you—from being a shorthand-typist cum secretary and mixing with our clients you will in future be a copy-typist and remain in the back room. That also, I'm afraid, involves reverting to the copy-typist salary scale. But, all in all, I hope you'll agree we've bent over backwards to—er—accommodate you."

My God, Olga thought—bent over backwards. She wondered what they'd have done if they'd stayed upright —branded her with a scarlet letter as in the old days? And if they'd leant forward it would probably have meant the thumbscrew and the rack at least.

She didn't, of course, say any of this. She'd learnt a lot since the start of her pregnancy. She'd certainly look for another job. But it would be stupid to give up this one before she'd found the next. A small dinge in her personal pride simply didn't count at all in comparison with the other problems on her mind. Anyway, the question of finding digs came before finding another job.

She murmured something deliberately inaudible. It could have been a rude word just as easily as thanks. Before Mr. Medway could say 'Pardon?' she turned and walked quickly out of his office.

That Saturday Piggy searched her private drawer and found the card that Willie's Uncle Timothy had given her. It said *The Beeches, Henley* and at the top was a phone number. She went to the phone in the hall and rang the number.

A woman's voice—it somehow suggested an elderly housekeeper—answered and Piggy said, speaking very quietly, "Could you please ask Mr. Torr if it would be convenient for Piggy to call this afternoon?"

The woman's voice said, "I didn't catch the name." Piggy repeated it and the woman asked, "Could you spell it, please?" So Piggy spelled it and then the woman said suspiciously, "Are you sure you've got the right number?" But finally she asked Piggy to hold on and went away from the phone.

When she came back she said in quite a different tone of voice, "Mr. Torr says he'll be very pleased to see you, Miss Piggy, and would you like him to send the car for you—?"

"Oh no," Piggy said quickly. "Please thank him but I'll go by train—"

"Very well, Miss," the voice said. It added helpfully, "From Paddington, then—or you can get a bus via Slough and Maidenhead—or by steamer from Kingston, though that'll take longer—"

"It's all right—really," Piggy said. She was afraid Willie might come through the hall and guess whom she was talking to. "I'll just go by rail from Paddington."

So a couple of hours later and some thirty-five miles from the *kibbutz* Piggy stepped out of the train and asked a station official—the only one in sight—the way to The

Beeches. She followed the directions he gave her and after walking about half a mile up a gently sloping incline was faced by a drive lined with rhododendron bushes, around the roots of which an elderly gardener was doing leisurely things with a rake. At the top of the drive stood the sort of house a jigsaw-puzzler finds depicted when he has fitted in the last piece. It wasn't particularly large but it had Tudor beams and creeper and a lot of character.

Piggy walked up the drive in the warm afternoon sunlight and the garden behind the rhododendrons came into view. It too was just like what you saw on a jigsaw-puzzle. The old gardener touched his hat to Piggy and she smiled back at him and couldn't help thinking what a good clue that straw hat of his would have made if you'd been searching for that particular bit of the jigsaw. She also couldn't help thinking how wonderful it would have been to be born here instead of in The Blue Hound in Wortley Street near the Old Vic.

Mr. Torr must have seen her coming up the drive for he was waiting for her on the step, his white side-whiskers like cottonwool in the sunlight.

"Well hullo, Piggy," he said, "so you've changed your mind and come to tell me all about it?"

They shook hands and Piggy said, "I'd better warn you it's pretty complicated. I just hope I can make it sound sensible. I fought against coming for a long time but in the end I had to give in."

"Where would you like to talk?—inside or in the garden?"

"In the garden, please."

"You don't want to powder your nose or anything first?" Mr. Torr asked matter-of-factly.

" Not at the moment," Piggy said.

Mr. Torr turned and shouted up the hall in a surprisingly strong voice, " We'll be in the garden, Mrs. James." Then he took Piggy by the arm and marched her to a rustic seat under a copper beech. He set Piggy down and then sat down himself a little creakily. About a mile away through the trees Piggy could see a straight bit of river.

" It's lovely," she said.

" Boulter's Lock's down there," Mr. Torr told her. " You should have seen it on Ascot Sunday in the old days. Busiest lock on the Thames. My, did we look smart with our boaters and blazers and the girls twirling parasols. It's all changed now—for the worse, people will tell you. I'm not so sure. We gave very little thought in those days to the underdog. Young people nowadays seem to worry a lot about the underdog. But you didn't come here to listen to an old codger's moralisings. You came to talk about this young nephew of mine, didn't you?"

For a moment the horrible feeling of jealousy returned. She saw Olga and Willie sitting there, much closer together than she and Uncle Timothy were sitting. Then she pretended she had magical powers and with a wave of her wand she made Olga disappear and she herself took Olga's place beside Willie. She brought herself back to a more sensible frame of mind by saying inwardly, ' You stupid bitch, this may be grim but it isn't Grimm's Fairy Tales '.

" Yes," she said aloud. " I thought I'd got it all laid out neatly in my mind. Now I forget where to begin."

" We decided at our first meeting it would be better

for Willie if we withheld what's coming to him in the meantime, didn't we? If you changed your mind you were to let me know. Why not just go on from there, Piggy?"

"Well," Piggy said, "I think now that it might be better for Willie if he got it right away. You *did* say you'd take him into your business and bring him here to live with you, didn't you?"

"I mentioned the possibility," Mr. Torr said. "But just why have you changed your mind?"

"Well," Piggy said, "Willie's been—depressed of late. Maybe if something new happened it would give him a gee-up."

"Hmph," Mr. Torr said.

He cocked a look at Piggy and she felt he didn't think she was being very convincing. At that moment Mrs. James advanced across the lawn carrying a tray on which were two glasses and a bottle. She set the tray down on the seat between them and Mr. Torr said, "Oh Miss Piggy, I'd like you to meet my house-keeper Mrs. James."

Piggy said, "How do you do?" and Mrs. James, who was big-boned and angular but had a face, Piggy noticed, like a friendly moose, said, "Pleased to meet you, Miss Piggy—oh I forgot to tell you, there was another way you could have come, by Uxbridge and Bourne End—"

Then Mr. Torr said, "That'll be all right thank you, Mrs. James, you can bring the afternoon tea in half an hour."

When the housekeeper had gone, Mr. Torr filled the two glasses and as they sipped the sherry he smiled at her and said, "It's quite a trip down here from

158

Roxton Gate, Piggy—somehow I don't feel you made it just to tell me Willie's feeling a bit depressed."

"He's in love," Piggy said, the words coming out of her like a greyhond out of its trap.

"Oh?" Mr. Torr said. "May I ask if it's with you?"

"Good Lord, no," Piggy told him (she wished to God it had been). Now that she had got that over she found words coming more easily. She looked up at the house. "There'd be room for two more—or even three— wouldn't there?" she asked. "I mean—not just Willie—"

"Yes," Mr. Torr said, "I think we could manage that if the need arose." He felt a little surprised. He had concluded that Piggy was working for herself as well as for Willie and would have thought none the less of her for that. "But who is this girl Willie's in love with?"

"Her name's Olga—Olga Beloff."

"Is she a nice girl?" Mr. Torr asked. "Take your time please, Piggy—I want a considered opinion."

"Oh I don't need time," Piggy said. "She's wonderful. At the moment she's a bit nutty—but she's wonderful. She never thinks of herself. That's the trouble, you see. She—they—well, they've—"

She stopped in some confusion. She thought highly of Willie's uncle but she didn't know him well enough to feel sure what his reaction would be to what she still had to tell him.

"Willie's got her in the family way, is that it?" Mr. Torr asked. He might have been talking about the weather.

"Yes."

"Hmph. How do you like my sherry?"

" It's wonderful sherry, Mr. Torr."

He filled both glasses up again.

" Are they in love?"

" Yes."

" Are you quite sure?"

" Quite sure."

" Well, then, there's really no problem, is there?"

" Oh yes there is—a hell of a problem," Piggy said quickly. " You don't know Olga. They're terribly in love, both of them, and I think Willie's asked Olga to marry him. Probably over and over again. But she won't do it—"

" Even if she won't that needn't stop them living together—times have changed—"

" Yes, it does. Because she thinks he'd have to get a job and pinch and slave for years in order to keep three of them—and maybe more later—and that would be sure to kill his writing completely. That's the crazy way Olga's worked it out—"

" Just a moment," Mr. Torr said. " Do you mean that this girl Olga intends going off somewhere to have her baby—her's and Willie's—and then bring it up all on her own, just to relieve Willie of responsibility and leave him free to continue his writing—?"

" That's right. I said she was crazy."

" Humph," Mr. Torr said again. He sat silent for some time, staring at the gardener raking among the rhododendrons. " Joe's getting past it, he's only going through the motions," he said, shooting off on one of the momentary tangents she'd come to expect of him. " If Willie came here to live and joined me in the business he could write in his spare time. Do you think Olga would marry him on those terms?"

"I doubt it," Piggy said. "There's a bit more to it than that. It's not just a matter of spare time. There's the question of inspiration too—"

"You said it would be complicated—no one could accuse you of exaggerating," Mr. Torr said drily.

"It's Olga that's causing the complication," Piggy said. "Olga thinks if only Willie could find a decent plot he'd be half way to becoming another Shakespeare. Whether she's right or not doesn't really matter—she believes it and nobody could change her. She also believes that marriage would kill any chance Willie ever has of finding that plot because all his inspiration would dribble away in thinking up things for the family—"

"A job and spare time I can give him," Mr. Torr said. "But I can't find him a plot. That's not in my line. So where do we go from here—?"

"Probably nowhere," Piggy said. "But in view of everything I felt it only fair to change my mind and not stand in the way of Willie getting your offer. After all, it's just possible that if you, as Willie's only remaining relative, could meet both Olga and Willie and explain it to them, Olga might change her mind too. I don't think it's better than a hundred to one shot but one has to try everything. But you'll have to be terribly tactful about it, Mr. Torr. You have to throw the rule-book away when you're dealing with Olga."

"One doesn't usually have to be all that tactful when one's trying to give away something for nothing," Mr. Torr said. "This Olga must be an unusual girl."

"Oh she is. As well as being wonderful she's as pig-headed as be damned. Though you don't find that out

F   161

until she comes up against something she thinks really important. Well, I feel better having got that off my chest, even if—"

She stopped suddenly as if finding herself on the verge of an indiscretion.

" Even if what, Piggy—?"

" Even if I've absolutely no personal interest in it myself."

They sat silent for a moment. Then Mr. Torr said, " So you think it would be a good idea if I had a chat with Olga and Willie together? Tell me how you'd go about it, Piggy."

Mrs. James came out with a small folding table and accessories. She set out the table, spread a cloth and held up the sherry bottle to inspect it. The level had gone down considerably. Mrs. James took the bottle and the glasses away and Mr. Torr chuckled. " She thinks we've had enough sherry," he said. Mrs. James came back almost immediately carrying a tea-tray piled high with sandwiches, cut cake and brandy snaps.

An hour and a half later Mr. Torr and Piggy were still sitting under the beech tree. By then each felt they knew the other a lot better. Piggy had made up her mind that Willie's uncle was shrewd, kindly, generous —but no mug. She would have been surprised had she known that at that moment Mr. Torr was feeling a little sad. For he had sensed that Piggy herself was in love with Willie and that it must have taken a tremendous effort of will for her to come down here and try to promote Willie's marriage to someone else. Of all the sad things in this world, he reflected, surely the saddest is unrequited love.

Assuming that anything were to come of it—which seemed most unlikely—Mr. Torr would have preferred Piggy as a daughter-in-law. She would, he felt, have made Willie an uncommonly good wife. He doubted if this Olga woman could possibly make as good a one. For that reason he felt a slight prejudice against Olga, in spite of Piggy's expressed opinion—but he would try to keep an open mind. He would have liked to do something for Piggy, but young people nowadays were infernally difficult to do anything for. They had their own standards which often seemed peculiar to older people—but by God they stuck to them.

"I think I'll powder my nose now," Piggy said.

"Give Mrs. James a shout as you go in," Mr. Torr said. "She'll show you where."

He watched her go across the lawn. He thought, they're a lot more sensible nowadays. In my day a girl would just have sat there till she burst.

When Piggy returned she said, "Well, I must be getting back. I just hope it works. Mind you, I don't think it will—but it's only right to give them the chance, no matter how slim it is. I don't suppose we'll meet again, Mr. Torr—I was only a sort of self-appointed go-between. Now I've gone between and my job's finished. I thanked Mrs. James for a lovely afternoon tea. And thank you for listening to me so patiently. I'll bet you never came across such a jumble-up in all your life before."

"Human beings come in an infinite variety," Mr. Torr said. "It was good of you to try to explain Olga's special brand to me. And now, if you like I'll get Joe to change into his chauffeur's uniform and drive you back to London—though honestly I wouldn't advise it.

He's shocking in traffic and the car hasn't been out of the garage for months. I don't drive myself and when I go up to town I go by train. That shows what I think of Joe's driving. However, if you care to risk it—"

"Thanks, I won't," Piggy said, laughing. "Anyway I bought a return."

He walked down the drive with her. At the gate she turned and looked back at the house—a little longingly, he fancied.

"Remember, Mr. Torr—you musn't mention my name—you don't even know me—"

"I'll remember," he promised.

He watched her go away towards the station. She looked attractive and as neat as a new pin in her mini-skirt. Good legs, too. Nowadays young fellows didn't have to do a lot of manual research to discover a girl had legs. And inside she seemed as nice as out. If this Olga's half as good, he reflected, Willie'll be damned lucky. He had never thought of Willie as a Casanova. Young dog, he must have got something.

I shouldn't feel sorry for Piggy, he thought then. Young people are never sad—not young people who feel young. Nor old people who feel old. The really sad ones were the old people who feel young underneath the wrinkles and stiff joints and double chins. Like himself.

He turned and went slowly back up the drive . . .

That evening, after dinner at the *kibbutz*, Piggy said to Max, "Please take me out somewhere, Max—to the pictures, for a drink, anywhere."

He looked at her in surprise because the request was out of character.

164

"I'm terribly sorry—I've arranged to play billiards with Ted. Will some other time do—?"

"Of course," she told him. "It doesn't matter—it doesn't matter at all."

SEVEN

THE TIME had come, Piggy decided, to announce her pregnancy to the *kibbutz*. If she waited much longer it would announce itself.

She chose Sunday at lunch time as the occasion. Everyone was there except Olga and Willie. Olga now spent most of her spare time at weekends searching for suitable digs. Usually Willie went along to help, though, as Olga pointed out, it really wasn't his worry—he wouldn't be moving his quarters.

Piggy said quite casually, " You remember the nursery scheme? Well, I think we should go ahead with it."

" But why?" Sue asked.

" My father left me a little money. I wouldn't mind paying the lion's share of the expense."

Sue said, " But we don't need it at the moment. Anyway, if it's a *kibbutz* promotion we should all subscribe equally."

Denise was looking at Piggy.

" Piggy! You're not—?"

" Up the shute?" Piggy said. " It may raise a laugh but as a matter of fact I am."

"Good God, it's getting to be a habit," Denise said. "We girls need a course in Pelmanism. Or the chemists should get back to the drawing-board or something. When did you know?"

"About the same time as Olga. I thought I'd let you recover from the first knock-down before I delivered a second."

After that everyone took it calmly. Except Max. Max said, "It's mine, isn't it—?"

"Yes," Piggy told him gently. "It couldn't be any-one else's. But don't worry. This one'll be a *kibbutz* baby. I'll pop it into the nursery." She added, "If we decide to have a nursery."

She couldn't help noticing that Max looked relieved. Unreasonably, she felt a little hurt at his relief.

"Well," Sue said, "there's not much doubt about that now, is there? It makes me feel like a loafer among workers—not being pregnant, I mean. You all right, Denise?"

"Okay up to the moment of going to press," Denise said. "We'd better start issuing hourly bulletins."

"Seriously," Sue said. "let's go into committee right now. There are a couple of things to discuss. First, the nursery scheme. Then we'll soon need a new girl member to replace Olga when she goes. It's no harm to plan ahead. We want to be careful who we get in." She remembered then that Willie was absent. "Maybe we should wait for Willie to be here," she said.

They talked that over for a while and decided to go ahead without Willie. They felt sure he would fall in with anything they decided on—at the moment he seemed unable to settle to discuss anything. Besides, they had a quorum without him.

"I second Sue's proposal that we go into committee,"
Ted said. "And I propose Sue as chairman."

"I second that," Denise said.

"Agreed," everyone murmured.

"I appreciate your confidence," Sue said. "Well then,
hands up all those in favour of having our own
nursery?"

Everybody's hand went up except Piggy's.

"What about you, Piggy?" Sue asked.

"I've declared an interest," Piggy said. "I'm not en-
titled to vote."

"Oh don't be silly, of course you are. If you want a
nursery, stick up your hand."

"You bet I want it," Piggy said and held up her
hand.

"Passed unanimously," Sue said. "Well, it seems
we're to have a nursery. It can only be on the top floor
and the expense is to be borne equally by all members
of the *kibbutz*—we can take those two points for granted,
it's not worth putting them to the meeting. Next question is, how much are we prepared to spend? Or rather
how much can we afford?"

"If we're doing it at all, let's do it properly," Ted
said. "We don't want to be mean about it—"

"At the same time, we'd better put a limit on the
expenditure," Tubby said. "You can run yourselves into
five or six hundred quid these days as easy as winking.
We don't want that. On the other hand, if it goes
beyond cash in hand, we could probably get a bank
loan. I think I could fix it with the launderettes' bank.
It's a pretty good account and the bank manager treats
me like I was important to him."

After discussion they decided to try to finance it from

their own resources and not to seek outside help in the meantime. They agreed on a figure and deputed Sue and Ted to make arrangements and supervise the carrying out of the work, but not to go beyond the figure without referring back to the others. In a way they could all supervise the work—it was only a matter of running upstairs at any time to see how it was going on.

" So much for the nursery, then," Sue said. " There's still the matter of co-opting a new girl member in the *kibbutz*. Maybe we'd better lay down general rules when we're at it, for sooner or later somebody else will drop out. Any ideas?"

Denise said she knew a buyer in the store called Jill who lived with her parents but wasn't getting on any too well with them. Denise thought Jill would definitely be interested—

" Measurements, please," Tubby said.

" Oh around thirty-six twenty-four thirty-six," Denise said. " And everything in its place—"

" Colouring?"

" She varies. At the moment she's blonde. But she's an obliging soul. I'm sure she'd change to suit."

" Pretty?"

" Oh my, yes. I'm not saying she's another Olga. But she's gone in for one or two beauty competitions and finished well up."

" Look," Tubby said, " all this is very well, but seeing's believing. Maybe we'd better do as Sue suggested and lay down a general rule for all applicants, male and female. Why don't we interview them before acceptance? After all one of us might take a scunner against an applicant for some personal quirk of taste and that would ruin the whole thing. We've never had a member that wasn't popular with everyone in the *kibbutz*. We want to keep it that way. Another thing, we want to make sure they'll join in the nursery scheme. Or one of them might be a bad mixer and refuse to fall in with rota arrangements or in some other way fall below the required standard. We want to make sure about things like that before we let them in."

It seemed a reasonable enough suggestion. After a short discussion it was agreed to make it permanent procedure that every new applicant must be interviewed by the whole *kibbutz* before being co-opted. There'd be nothing formal or stiff about it. He or she would just be asked in for a chat over a cup of tea. If opinion was unanimously favourable and all questions were answered satisfactorily the new member would be in. If there was even one dessentient, the applicant would be turned down as tactfully and painlessly as possible. After all it would be much kinder to turn down an applicant than have to expel him or her after acceptance.

When the meeting finally broke up everybody agreed they'd handled the agenda in a terrifically businesslike way. They all felt reasonably sure that Olga's coming departure would not destroy the *kibbutz* as at one time had seemed not improbable.

Piggy was having a quiet weep. She didn't really know why. She had been a little sick that morning—maybe it was all part of the same thing. Things were happening inside her that had knocked all her usual timetables for six. It was like exchanging one curse for another.

It was during lunch break at the boutique; Sue was at the counter outside and Piggy was alone with her out-of-sorts-ness. It was just this moment that Uncle

Ikey chose to poke his flattened face round the door. It was very rarely he did this. But once in a blue moon he would look in to ask if his staff was comfortable and had everything they wanted.

Piggy took out her hankie quickly and blew her nose and pretended she hadn't been crying. But Mr. Rottger had seen.

"What is this, please?" he said, clucking his tongue and looking really worried. "One of my young ladies crying. This is not good, not good at all."

Mr. Rottger's rotund body followed his flattened face into the staff room. His fighting weight had once been welter but he was a lot more than that now. He came forward with an awkward little shuffle as if he had no right to be there and sat down opposite Piggy at the table.

"I'm just being silly," Piggy said, sniffing and putting her hankie away. "It's nothing—you probably know how emotionally unstable women are at times, Mr. Rottger."

"Nobody cries without they have a reason," Mr. Rottger said, "this much I know. There is something wrong with my boutique, maybe? Then tell me, please, and we will change it, no matter what it is—"

"No, no, the boutique's fine—as a matter of fact, I love it," Piggy said. She never knew how to conduct a conversation with Mr. Rottger. It wasn't that he was a particularly elegant talker, just one you could somehow never get the better of. "I don't know why I was crying—maybe it's just a lot of small things getting on top of me—"

"Small things?" Mr. Rottger said. He sat thinking that over for a moment or two. "You think to yourself, maybe, why doesn't this fat old Jew man with the flattened face go away and not bother me? Why can't he stick his big flat nose into someone else's business, yes?" He shrugged and rose to his feet. "This I can understand any young lady thinking—so I will go now, Miss Piggy." He was quite cunning, was Mr. Rottger. He had worked it out that this was the best way to get Piggy to tell him what was wrong.

"No—don't go," Piggy cried. "Please, Mr. Rottger —whatever I was crying about, it certainly wasn't you. You can't possibly have made anyone cry in your whole life. If I was crying about any one thing in particular, it was because I'll soon have to leave—"

"Oi, Oi, what is this?" Mr. Rottger exclaimed in genuine alarm, sitting down again. "You are going to leave me? No, I will not believe it. What have I done, please—?"

"It's not what you've done, Mr. Rottger—it's what I've done," Piggy said. "You can't have a girl with a big tummy working in a boutique—"

"Ha!" Mr. Rottger exclaimed and slapped the table. "Now we are getting somewhere. You are making a baby, yes—?"

"I'm making a baby, yes," Piggy said. "I was going to tell you just before it became obvious—which could be anytime now. I—I wanted to stay on as long as possible."

She saw that Mr. Rottger was gesticulating at her across the table, his elbows tucked into his sides and his hands fluttering in the neighbourhood of his cauliflower ears.

"And for this you think I should put you out?" he demanded. "What have I ever done to you that such an opinion of me you should have? Because my face is punched flat—because I am no oil painting—does that make me an ogre—?"

"Please, Mr. Rottger," Piggy said. "I didn't say you'd put me out—it's bad you should think this," (in conversation with Uncle Ikey she sometimes found herself speaking a little like him). "I meant I felt I'd have to go. A pregnant counter-hand isn't exactly a good advertisement for the sort of slimline fashions we sell—"

"Then a new line we will add," Mr. Rottger said. "'Modes for the Young Marrieds'—'Clothes for the Careless'—'Fashions for the Fertile'—call it anything you like. We will have a special rack at the back of the shop—and like hot buns it will go, you will see. How do you think of that, Miss Piggy—?"

Piggy suddenly felt like crying again. "I think perhaps you are the kindest man I know," she said.

The condition and texture of Mr. Rottger's face were such that it was impossible for him to blush. Nevertheless he made a very fair attempt at it.

"Kindness—pah!" he said. "This is business, not kindness. I know on which side of my bread the butter is. I will tell you something. How long have you two young ladies been with me now?—nearly two years it is. I am no fool, please. I know what is going on. Previous girls I have had—not young ladies. They have stolen from me—fifty pence here, a pound there, maybe a dress the other place. I say to myself, this I must put up with, it goes with the business. Then you two came—and very soon I know you are different. Not only do you not rob me, you bring me business. Miss Beloff and Miss Mont are good customers. It is better than an advertisement to have such pretty girls walking about in my clothes—people must sometimes ask them, where did you get those hot pants, they look so well on you? They are your personal friends—this I know. So I tell myself, if my young ladies give these personal friends an occasional dress at cost price, or even a little below cost price, I will not think any worse of them. Just the same, I watch—you do not know, but I watch. And what do I find?—I find that your friends are paying the same price as anyone else—"

"But that's no credit to us," Piggy said. "Neither Olga nor Denise would let us cheat even if we wanted to—"

"Please do not interrupt when I am making a long speech," Mr. Rottger said. "'At last,' I say to myself, 'at last you can take life easier, Barney Rottger, because behind you are two young ladies you can trust.' And now one of them tells me, because I am having a baby I must leave. What nonsense is this, please? What a trifle is having a baby compared to being honest. These things happen—should I now know? Do you think I sleep in one room, Rebecca in another? This you think, Miss Piggy?"

Piggy couldn't quite follow his logic but he seemed to be waiting for an answer so she said, "No, Mr. Rottger, this I didn't think."

"Well then, Miss Piggy, please let us have no more foolish talking about leaving. No matter how big you get, you will continue to work as long as you feel comfortable. Then, when the time comes, you will take a fortnight off, or a month—whatever is necessary—on full pay, of course. While you are gone Barney Rottger will have to work harder, which is a pity. But after you have had your baby you will come back so I can take life easy again. You will do this, please—?"

"Yes," Piggy said gratefully, "Yes, of course I'll come back like a shot—"

Mr. Rottger suddenly dealt himself a slap on the side of the head.

"I forget about the baby. Arrangements must be made for the baby to be looked after while you are at work. Why not bring it to the boutique each day and Rebecca will look after it? She is not a genius but she has a kindly nature and if she needs you she has only to run downstairs—"

"It's a wonderful idea," Piggy said, "but I've already made plans for that—"

"Well, then, a small rise in salary might be no harm," Mr. Rottger said. "We will see about that, yes? Then there is only left the matter of having the baby. It is better to have it in a nursing home, I think. I do not know how your friend—the father of the baby —is placed financially, but if there are difficulties, I might be able to help a little there, too—"

This time Piggy could not restrain a small sob of gratitude.

"There's no difficulty about that either," she said. "My father left me enough money to start the baby off—"

"Well then, everything is lovely in the garden," Uncle Ikey said. "So there will be no more crying—?"

"No more crying," Piggy said.

Even as she said it another tear somehow escaped and rolled down her cheek.

"Goodness me, goodness me," Mr. Rottger said. He felt then that all his talk had been for nothing. There wasn't a thing he could do to help. For this, he saw

175

now, wasn't a money matter, it was an affair of the heart. Someone—as he phrased it to himself—is not in love with someone who should be, or is in love with someone who should not be.

Barney Rottger, he told himself, you have probed as far as is good. With your big clumsy fingers you will only make the hurt worse if you probe further. He rose to his feet.

"Please," he said, "do not cry any more, Miss Piggy. It hurts me to see young ladies cry. Just remember to let me know if anything I can ever do to help."

"I'll remember," Piggy said. His flattened nose reminded her ever so slightly of Willie's. She felt like planting a kiss on it but restrained herself because she knew any such assault would have sunk Uncle Ikey without trace in a sea of embarrassment. She just added, "I'll try not to cry any more—I promise."

At that moment Sue burst into the staff room exclaiming, "Hey—what's keeping you, Farthingale?" Then she saw Mr. Rottger and stopped suddenly. "Oh, I'm sorry—"

"It's all right, please," Mr. Rottger said. "It's my fault—we were talking business, that is all." Suddenly he became embarrassed as if he had been caught in something shameful. "I go now," he announced, and went.

"What was all that in aid of?" Sue asked. "You've been crying, haven't you?"

"I told him I was pregnant," Piggy explained. "He was so sweet about it I cried."

"Logical enough," Sue said. "Do you want to cry some more?—or are you coming to the counter? I'll do a bit longer if you like—"

"No, I'm coming," Piggy told her. At the door she paused. "Why are women such bloody fools?"

"Search me," Sue said. "But it's a hell of a good question."

Sue and Ted got on with the nursery job with commendable promptitude and zeal. Within a couple of days workmen were in the *kibbutz* sawing and hammering like mad on the top floor. In spite of the noise it turned out to be a relatively minor operation. There already was a bathroom of sorts up there; after flat sides had been fitted round the bath and a new plug and chromium chain put in it looked really modern and natty.

No new plumbing was needed, but it was found necessary to divide the one big room with a hardboard partition. When the joiners went, the painters came in, but only for a couple of days. The carpet and curtains were the most expensive items but Denise managed to get these wholesale from her store.

The furniture, as it turned out, was a cakewalk. Denise got Max to drive her down to Strawberry Hill and collected from her home an old cot—her own—explaining to her mother that she wanted it for a charity thing (which in a sense was true enough). Ted and Max, who were good with their hands, supplied most of the rest. They bought do-it-yourself kits—charged, of course, to the *kibbutz* as a whole—and within a fortnight had put together and painted a cupboard, wardrobe, table and chairs of a quite professional appearance and solidity.

Very little new linen was required—there was already enough in the *kibbutz* to go round. A good secondhand bed for Mrs. Williams was picked up cheaply at an auction. If the girls noticed in shop windows any other odds and ends that looked a bargain and they thought might be useful they went in and bought them, afterwards charging them to the nursery fund. In the end it all came to far less than anyone had thought possible.

Mrs. Williams herself evolved almost visibly from the status of cleaner to that of nanny. For the moment she remained a cleaner and wouldn't get her rise in wages till the baby arrived but she began to trail clouds of future glory. She came to live in like a boxer going into strict training for a title fight. Sometimes Piggy would go up and have long chats with her. Mrs. Williams was quite an authority on babies, having, as she put it, dropped half a dozen of the little buggers herself. The first time, she admitted, was a bit of a facer because of the unusage, but after that it was just like shelling peas.

All that could be done had been done. The next move was up to Piggy. From the speed at which everything had been rushed through she might have been about to begin labour at any moment. Actually the increase in her waistline was barely even visible yet. There was, she supposed, something about first babies that makes even those only remotely concerned begin planning far ahead, as if it was the Olympic Games or a new aeroplane. Subsequent arrivals would probably cause less fuss, though she doubted if she'd ever reach the blasé pea-shelling stage claimed by Mrs. Williams. Anyway, she felt she'd probably make do with one.

Olga had wanted to subscribe to the nursery, but the other *kibbutzers*, after consideration, had declined the offer, saying it wouldn't be fair as she wouldn't be using it. She had discovered two 'digs' that seemed possibilities and was now trying to decide between them. She expected to be gone from the *kibbutz* in about a fortnight and in the meantime, although still in it, was not really any longer of it.

It was a rainy Sunday afternoon and most of the *kibbutzers* were in. Olga was knitting baby clothes. Early that afternoon Piggy had made a phone call to Henley suggesting that the occasion might be propitious.

When a ring came to the door it was Olga who chanced to answer it. The rain coated, white-whiskered old gentleman on the doorstep asked her if he could see Willie Torr.

"Yes, I'll get him," Olga said. "Won't you please come in?"

"Thank you," the old gentleman said. "Just say it's his Uncle Timothy."

While he was hanging up his wet raincoat in the hall he noticed that the girl was shoo-ing several young people out of a sitting-room so that he and Willie would have it to themselves. As he sat and waited he thought, the young dog seems to have surrounded himself with pretty girls. First there was Piggy and now there's this one. He liked the look of her very much and had to admit that she even outshone Piggy. He wondered if by any chance she was the one Willie had got pregnant. He hadn't noticed any signs of it yet in her figure but it would have been rude to have a good stare. If that's the one, he thought, Willie's even luckier than I imagined—a girl like that could pick and choose anyone she wanted.

179

Willie came in and they shook hands.

"Look, Willie," Uncle Timothy said, "I want you to do me a favour—"

"Of course, anything I can, Uncle Timothy," Willie said. "But first, wouldn't you like a cup of tea or something—?"

"I'd take a drop of sherry if you have it," Uncle Timothy said.

Willie rummaged round and produced a bottle and poured two glasses. It looked like the same bottle Piggy had served Uncle Timothy from on his first visit. Whatever else they get up to, he thought, they're not big drinkers.

"Now," Willie asked, "what can I do for you, Uncle Timothy?"

"Well," Uncle Timothy said, "it's like this. I'm getting on and I've nobody behind me in the business. It's been worrying me a lot lately. I wondered if you'd care to come in with me. You know what my photography business is like. It's not madly exciting but it's got some pretensions to being artistic and it's a reasonable living. Also, you'd still have plenty of time for your writing. It's really a matter of seeing that the work's done rather than doing it yourself. You could shape it to suit and when you've found your feet there's no reason why you shouldn't cut your week to something under thirty hours. Well, what do you say, Willie?"

Willie sat and pondered. When he pondered his bent nose made him look like Rodin's Thinker. Watching him, Uncle Timothy thought, it really is different nowadays. In my day a young fellow would have jumped at a cushy offer like that. But now they think differently— they think more about self-expression than making money. He wondered what else Willie was thinking about.

"It's a marvellous offer and I'm truly grateful," Willie said at length. "You're sure it's what you want? I mean, you're not just doing it because I haven't made much of a go of things—?"

"Look, Willie," Uncle Timothy said, "I wouldn't know whether you're making a go of things or not. We've all our own notions about what constitutes a go. I only know I'm an old man and I need help and you're my last remaining relative. Isn't that a real enough motive without looking for imaginary ones?"

"Ye-es," Willie said. He sat for a moment longer before he came to his decision. "I accept, Uncle Timothy. And I'll do my very best not to let you down."

"I know you will, Willie. Otherwise I wouldn't have asked you.

"Maybe you thought I'd baulk at the long journey down to Henley and back daily," Willie said. "But I don't mind that—"

"Just a minute, Willie," Uncle Timothy cut in. "You couldn't possibly look after the business from here—I can tell you at once that's not practicable. You'd have to come down and live with me at The Beeches—"

"I couldn't do that," Willie said quickly. "I'm sorry but I simply couldn't—"

"Why not?"

"Well—there's someone here—I've got to be around—"

"You mean, you've got a girl?" Uncle Timothy said. "Well, why not marry her and bring her down too? The house is big enough—"

"She wouldn't go," Willie said.

"If she won't go, that lets you out, doesn't it? You don't have to hang around—"

"But I'm in love with her," Willie said. "I want to hang around. She'll be leaving here soon for another address in London, but even when she goes, I'll still hang around her. She doesn't know that yet. But I've made up my mind. Just as close as I can get."

"Is she in love with you?"

"I don't know. I only know she won't marry me. There's—there's another reason why I have to hang around. I—I've made her pregnant, Uncle Timothy."

"You've made her pregnant but she won't marry you?" Uncle Timothy said. (It surprised Willie how easily his uncle seemed to accept the pregnancy bit.) "I don't understand. When women get caught they usually want to catch the catcher. She must be an unusual young woman."

"She is," Willie said. "She's Russian."

Uncle Timothy had to think for a moment or two what was the next step in the manoeuvre.

He said, "Look, Willie—would it be possible for me sometime to meet this girl for myself? It might clarify things a bit—you never know—"

"You can meet her now—she hasn't left yet," Willie said. "Do you really want to? I can tell you, you won't make her change her mind if that's what you're hoping. Once she's made it up, nobody can—"

"Just the same, I'd like to meet her," Uncle Timothy said.

"I'll see if she'll come down now. Help yourself to another sherry while you're waiting."

Willie left the room and Uncle Timothy poured himself another glass of sherry. The bottle was nearly empty now. Willie was gone some time and Uncle Timothy concluded he must be having an argument with his girl.

After a while Willie came back with the girl. It was the same girl who had let Uncle Timothy in.

"This is Olga Beloff—my Uncle Timothy," Willie said.

This time they shook hands and then they all sat down, Willie and Olga on the couch facing Uncle Timothy's armchair. Olga had been in attractive slacks when she opened the door to him, now she was in an even more attractive mini-frock—so it was changing into something more formal to meet him that had kept her. Uncle Timothy sat for a moment quite openly sizing her up. Her pregnancy didn't seem to show at all yet. She was so pretty he could quite happily have sat just looking at her for the next couple of hours. He decided, Willie's really got himself something here. At first glance she appeared as sophisticated as a girl could be, then he looked again and became aware of a sort of elfin innocence beneath the sophistication. Uncle Timothy in his day had known a lot about women. He decided, this one's different. It's not just the fact that she's Russian. He remembered Piggy had said of her—'you'll have to throw the rule-book away when dealing with Olga.'

"My nephew tells me you're Russian, Miss Beloff," he said.

Olga hesitated before replying. She even, Uncle Timothy noted, blushed slightly. With a sudden flash of perception he guessed that her Russian origin was some sort of joke she'd been playing on her friends.

183

She seemed to be in a trifling dilemma and Uncle Timothy waited with interest to see how she would deal with it.

"Please call me Olga," she said. "I'm—I'm not really Russian at all. That was just a joke—actually I'm English with a dash of Swedish." She saw Willie staring at her. "Sorry, Willie. Everyone seemed to get such a kick out of having a Russian girl about the place I hadn't the heart to disillusion them. It was all right among ourselves but it wouldn't be fair to keep it up with your uncle."

Willie grinned.

"You're still Olga Beloff," he said. "That's what matters."

Uncle Timothy recalled that Piggy had been very definite these two were in love. She was right about Willie—no doubt about that at all, quite apart from Willie's acknowledgement of the fact. But Olga?—Uncle Timothy wasn't sure yet. Obviously she liked him—but liking was a long way from loving.

"Has Willie told you about my suggestion?" he asked.

"Yes," Olga said.

"What do you think of it?"

"It's a marvellous chance for Willie provided he has enough time to write."

"He'll have plenty of time to write," Uncle Timothy said. "You'll come too, of course—that's understood."

She looked at him quickly.

"Oh no," she said, "oh no, I can't do that."

"Why not? You're going to bear his child, aren't you?"

"Yes," she said. "But don't you understand about

184

Willie? He's got the makings of a fine writer—I know he has. It's just that he hasn't found the right thing to write about yet. One day he will—and then everyone'll know what I know. But he's got to have peace of mind to bring that about. I know Willie—if he had a wife and child hanging round his neck he'd lavish all his attention on them and neglect everything else. He can't help it. It's just the way he's made. Oh yes, it would be very nice for the wife and child—but what about Willie—? What about that masterpiece he's going to write—?"

Suddenly Willie gave a sort of strangled moan. Uncle Timothy looked at him in surprise and some anxiety. He had never heard Willie make a sound like that before.

" Christ," Willie almost shouted, " why are you so bloody stupid? Bugger my masterpiece. I can't live without you. Can't you get that into your lovely, gorgeous, stupid head? Do I have to spell it out to you? *I—can't —live—without—you—!*"

Olga looked at Uncle Timothy. Her face was really distressed now.

" You see?" she said. " He's that way now and there's only one of us. When the baby comes along, he'd be twice as bad. What chance would he have to think of a plot for his book?"

Uncle Willie couldn't find words to reply for a moment. You'll have to throw the rule-book away, Piggy had said—by heavens, she was right!

He said, " But as the father of the child, Willie's got a responsibility—"

" No," Olga said. " It wasn't his fault. You see, when we started the *kibbutz* we all knew what we were taking on—the girls as well as the men, I mean. We did it with our eyes open because it seemed a good idea—"

The word *kibbutz* was new to Uncle Timothy. He couldn't remember Piggy having mentioned it.

"Tell me about the *kibbutz*," he said.

Olga told him then—not everything, but quite enough to enable him to fill in the blanks himself. And as he listened, Uncle Timothy felt an idea begin to take shape in his mind. It came to him out of the blue and had nothing to do with plans laid beforehand. It was a wonderful idea—and like all wonderful ideas, absurdly simple.

He looked at Olga and said, "Tell me, Olga—tell me truly—do you love my nephew Willie?"

He saw then she was having some sort of struggle with herself. In each blue eye a big tear appeared, then very slowly the two tears brimmed over and ran down her cheeks. He heard Willie make the odd strangled sound again.

Then Olga said in a small voice, "Yes—I love Willie very much. If I didn't, I couldn't let him go."

At first it didn't make sense to Uncle Timothy but when he thought of it for a moment it made a lot of sense. And then he came out with his wonderful idea.

"It seems to me all the trouble stems from Willie's inability to find a plot. Why doesn't he write about the *kibbutz*?"

They both stared at him as if he had said something apocalyptic. Then they stared at each other.

"Christ!—he's hit it!—*he's hit it!*" Willie shouted.

Olga just murmured, "Oh Willie!"

"Some people would hate it and others would love it," Uncle Timothy said. "But I think it would make an interesting book—provided you just told the facts

186

without putting in any fiction. Boys and girls living together—you can't get a subject with greater common appeal than that. I don't know if you'd call it a plot but at least it's a theme. They don't seem to go much for plots nowadays anyway."

He saw that Olga and Willie had risen and were hugging each other and jumping up and down like two footballers who have co-operated in scoring a goal. Willie's book, if he writes it, will have a happy ending too, he thought. They seemed to have forgotten him so he poured himself the last of the sherry and drank it quickly. It was really a toast to himself for having had his inspiration. In one sentence he seemed to have solved all their problems.

It was Olga who stopped jumping about first.

"Hey," she said, "we're forgetting about the baby. It'll wonder if we're having an earthquake or something . . ."

Ten minutes later, as Olga and Willie were seeing Uncle Timothy out, they chanced to meet Piggy coming down the stairs.

Olga said, "Oh, this is one of our other *kibbutzers*— I'd like you to meet her. Miss Piggy Farthingale—Mr. Torr, Willie's uncle."

Piggy and Uncle Timothy shook hands and murmured, "How do you do?" like strangers meeting for the first time.

Olga, still bubbling with excitement, said, "Uncle Timothy's just thought of a plot for Willie—isn't it wonderful—?"

Piggy stared at Willie's uncle. He shrugged and told her, "I don't know where it came from, it just came."

They chatted for a few moments and then Uncle

Timothy said, " Well, I must be going—I've got a train to catch—"

" Have you far to go, Mr. Torr?" Piggy asked, poker-faced.

" Quite a bit—to Henley, actually."

" It's still raining, I'll get Max to run you down," Piggy said. " Hold on a jiffy, Mr. Torr—"

" You musn't trouble—please—"

But Piggy had already run off to find Max.

Later, driving down to Henley with Max, Uncle Timothy mused, if you manage to make two people happy out of three I suppose you're not doing so badly. But it would have been so much nicer if it could have been three.

Olga got a certain pardonable pleasure from sending in her resignation to Mr. Medway.

She and Willie were married in the Roxton Register Office a week later. The remaining *kibbutzers* and Uncle Timothy and Mrs. Williams filled the quite small room. All the girls looked very smart and Mrs. Williams had on a new hat that was like a flaming brazier in the dingy surroundings.

As a wedding present the other *kibbutzers* had bought Olga and Willie a week's honeymoon in Paris. So after the civil ceremony they all bundled into taxis as far as the air terminal and then went on by bus to Heathrow to see them off.

There was much throwing of confetti and chaffing about the way Olga and Willie had let down the ideals of the *kibbutz*. But there was no real malice in the chaffing. After all, as Tubby pointed out, the term freedom included the freedom to revert to being a stinking *bour-*

geois if that was what you really wanted. It took all sorts to make a world.

Denise said, as they watched the plane take off, " Bless them, did you see how they looked at each other? That was *really bourgeois*. I've a feeling they're going to be terrifically happy."

Uncle Timothy said, " When they get settled in at The Beeches you must all come down and we'll have a party to celebrate."

Mrs. Williams remarked, " They'll be getting it legal now—not as that makes it any more fun in my experience. Still, it doesn't matter how you gets it just as long as you gets it."

" They were both good *kibbutzers* till they got bitten by the bug," Sue said. " We'll miss them—but we've got to keep looking forward. Whatever we do, we musn't weaken. Next thing is to find another couple to take their places."

Max and Ted hardly said anything because they were so sad at Olga leaving the *kibbutz*.

Piggy didn't say much either.

It was weeks later. At breakfast in the *kibbutz* this morning there were two new members—Jill and Harry. Jill had been sponsored by Denise and Harry by Ted, and both had passed their interviews to the satisfaction of the *kibbutzers*. They had just spent their first night in the *kibbutz* in the room vacated by Olga and Willie.

They looked cool and groovy and self-assured but the others realised they must be feeling like a couple of non-league players suddenly signed on by Manchester United. Doubtless they knew the basic skills of the game but the stadium was new to them. The old hands, with sympathetic tact, were diverting attention away from the newcomers until they found their feet.

Denise said brightly, " Oh Tubby—I nearly forgot. Mummy wants me to take you down some Saturday or Sunday afternoon to Strawberry Hill. What'll I tell her—?"

" What's in it for me?" Tubby asked.

" Meringues."

" Goody—tell your mother I'll go."

" First fine afternoon at the weekend, then. Just don't expect a bacchanalia, that's all. We'll have tea on the lawn and look at the swans "—Denise giggled—" while Mummy sits wondering if I've ever slept with you."

Everybody laughed, including Jill and Harry.

Across the table Piggy laughed with the others but as she did so something inside her seemed to turn over. She thought desperately, I won't get tired of it—I won't, I won't. There must be happiness somewhere along the way—there must be completeness.

Her parents Fred and Vicky certainly hadn't found it and at the moment she didn't seem likely to find it herself—but it must be somewhere. Maybe Olga and Willie would stumble on it down there in Henley.

Maybe even yet it could be found here in the *kibbutz*. It wasn't impossible. Oh God, she found herself praying, please make it possible—at least, God, please let my baby be happy even if you can't manage it for me . . .